I0451952

COURTSHIP OF A SESSION WRESTLER

THE WISE MAN AND THE WARRIOR BOOK 1

L.A. GOODYEAR

Copyright © 2021 Larry Goodyear
All cover art copyright © 2021 Larry Goodyear
All Rights Reserved

This is a work of fiction. Names, places, characters and incidents are either the product of the author's imagination or are used fictitiously, and any resemblance to any actual persons, living or dead, businesses, organizations, events or locales is entirely coincidental.

No part of this book may be reproduced or transmitted in any form or by any means, electronic or mechanical, including photocopying, recording, or by any information storage and retrieval system, without permission in writing from the author.

Publishing Coordinator – Sharon Kizziah-Holmes
Cover Design – Jaycee DeLorenzo

Paperback-Press
an imprint of A & S Publishing
A & S Holmes, Inc.

ISBN -13: 978-1-951772-26-0

DEDICATION

This is dedicated to all who have endured the pain of divorce and had to cope with the uncertainties that follow. I can't imagine what that's like for those who don't have Christ comforting them! *"A threefold cord is not suddenly broken,"* indeed. He is still with me, closer than a brother and keeping me upright.

"Eye has not seen, nor ear heard, nor has it entered into the heart of man the things that God has prepared for him." If this story tweaks the reader's imagination, causing him or her to consider a fraction of those possibilities, perhaps it will spark hope. I'd like that. Nothing is random for those who trust in Jesus, and nothing is too difficult for Him!

-Larry Allen Goodyear

ACKNOWLEDGMENTS

I'd like to thank Sharon Kizziah-Holmes of Paperback Press, without whom this would most likely never have been published. Her knowhow was critical in getting it done right, and she believed in me. I'd recommend her to any first-time writer!

My thanks also goes to J. C. DeLorenzo of Sweet 'n Spicy Designs. Her cover design based on a general description of what I envisioned is a sterling representation of the story within.

It was with my mother that I first shared my daydream; she persuaded me to put it in writing, so she could follow along as it grew. Boy, did it grow! This is only the first book of four so far, and a fifth is in progress. See what you started, Mom? Even though editing and publishing details have sidelined development for a time, I fully intend to get back to it so you can see what happens next! I won't leave you hanging.

Allen is based on my life, my fictional alter-ego, if anyone is wondering. *"To Him who is able to do exceedingly abundantly above all we ask or think; to Him be glory forever, amen."* My thinking can get pretty far out there, as you can see. If my God can top it, as this scripture indicates, then the life I lost might not define me in the end. May it be so! He gives me hope to carry on when I am sitting in the ruins of the life I thought I had. Whatever life I have left is His. He will determine if I have a future before He calls me home, and whether it matters in the end. Jesus Christ is my grubstake; I'm not gonna give Him up!

CHAPTER 1

The world we live in extols movers and shakers. They are exciting, capturing the imaginations of average working folks whose lives seem anything but extraordinary. The cycle of 'work, eat, sleep, repeat' isn't designed to unveil individual potential. When tragedy strikes, human potential can be unlocked; but it can just as easily be forever lost.

Allen Edwards was a case in point. The daily grind had taken its toll, wearing him down until he had little self-confidence left. Recently divorced after 38 years of marriage, nearing retirement age, it seemed life had passed him by and all he had built of it was invalidated. He had no inkling how God Almighty had set things in motion to repair his broken heart and give his life significance!

One day after work, he stopped at a convenience store for a soda, a treat for himself after his night shift. Upon entering the store, he took notice of the customer at the counter, her back to him as she faced the cashier. What struck him were her legs. She wore form-fitting insulated ski pants that did nothing to hide their shape. He was a red-blooded male with a special appreciation for lovely lady legs. Hers were spectacularly well proportioned!

She wore a parka with the hood down, a wealth of blond hair completely obscuring any glimpse of her face. She seemed about average height, though her fashionable high heel boots could have exaggerated her stature. He took in the view as the cashier called out a greeting and went on to get his drink.

She was turning from the counter when he was ready to check out. He finally saw her face. She looked to be about mid-40s, with delicate features and a somewhat pale complexion. Bright blue eyes caught his, so he averted his gaze before things got awkward.

In the course of the transaction, he turned a bit to see her as she left the store; however, she didn't leave. About two steps back, she stopped and stared at him unabashedly. When she saw him glance at her, she made no attempt to look away.

Unnerved, he completed his purchase and turned to leave. She was still there, still staring! He stepped up to ask her, "Is something wrong?"

"No, nothing's wrong. I think I recognize you, that's all," she replied. She had the most striking blue eyes he had ever seen.

He chuckled, "Not likely. I wouldn't forget your face!"

She smiled a crooked smile accentuated by dark red lipstick. "I would like to explain, if you don't mind. It could take some time. Could we go somewhere to talk privately?"

"Sure, I guess. Have you eaten yet?"

She had not. He suggested going to a drive-in where she could get breakfast and he could order dinner, having just gotten off work. They could eat in either vehicle, where they could talk. She agreed.

They pointed out their cars; he had his mom's van, while she drove a nice black and white retro-style Mustang. She followed him to Sonic and parked side by side, where he joined her in her car.

She placed their order, then turned to him. "I hope you don't think I make a habit of picking up men at gas stations, because I'm not like that, you know?"

He laughed, "I never thought you were. Besides, I approached you, remember? Even though I did because you were staring a hole through me. I gotta admit, that was a bit creepy."

"I'm sorry! It's just – I *do* have an explanation, but I need to ask: are you married?"

Looking down at his feet, he answered, "Not anymore. Are you?"

"No, never have been. What happened?"

"We married when we were both 18. I came from a stable home and she was abused. She was my first girlfriend and I was her second boyfriend, so neither of us had any experience dating. I couldn't believe a girl was paying attention to me. I fell hard!

"I was her ticket out of the abuse, though I still believe she loved me back then. We were married for almost forty years. She left three years ago. I was recently served with divorce papers, which finalized a month ago. Neither of us were seeing anyone else, to my knowledge. The court said we were incompatible, and at this point, I can't disagree."

"I'm sorry. Is there a chance of your reconciling?"

"That's not going to happen," he told this stranger, wondering why he did. "We started off, now that I think about it, at a drive-in, sipping milkshakes and talking for hours. We shared our personal thoughts, feelings and experiences. She became my best friend in the world. That lasted for decades. The divorce breached that trust. I'll never open myself up for that again, not with her, anyway."

"So, you weren't just divorced, you were also betrayed by your best friend."

He could feel those piercing blue eyes watching him. He looked up to see a tenderness there he found comforting. "I never thought of it like that. Guess that's why it hit me so hard, even though she's been gone three years."

There was a moment of silence before he spoke again, "Since we've established we're both not married and I'm spilling the story of my failed marriage like a wounded animal bleeding out, I guess introductions are in order," he said with a grin. "My name is Allen Edwards." He stuck his hand out.

She blushed and clasped his hand quickly, "Erin Adams. I should have introduced myself before I started asking personal questions."

"No problem. You just asked if I was married; it snowballed from there. It's nice to have someone to talk to. I didn't mean to unload on you."

At that point the food arrived. While he dug out a ten-spot, she produced a credit card, which the carhop ran. She waved off his money, stating he was only there at her request, so she had this.

They began to eat before he asked her, "Are you a local?"

Her mouth was full, so she shook her head.

"I didn't think so. You don't dress or act like a local. You're wearing some serious winter apparel for this climate."

"I'm a California girl. I got cold! Last night when I arrived, I went to Bass Pro and bought the warmest stuff I could find. Guess I'm outfitted for the Arctic now, but I'm sure glad I'm not there," she said with a broad grin. "I'm on my way to Chicago on business. I produce custom videos, have my own company in partnership with a friend of mine. What do you do to pay the bills?"

"I'm a caregiver. Folks with developmental disabilities live in their own rented homes, with staff provided to pass medications, transport them to appointments, and help them with household tasks like cooking and cleaning as needed. Basically, we help them fit into their community and guide their interactions with it."

"That sounds rewarding!" she enthused.

"It is, in that it makes a difference in the lives of the less fortunate. I make twelve dollars an hour, so the financial reward has definite limits."

"How do you live on that? If you don't mind my asking," she added.

"My parents moved in with us when Dad was diagnosed with non-alcoholic cirrhosis of the liver. He passed in 2007. Mom is still with me, seventy-six years old and barely getting around. I help her when she needs help, and she helps me with her Social Security Income. That's how we manage."

She kept him talking, showing more interest in his life than he could justify, but seemed genuinely interested in what he told her. She said little about herself. She traveled the world, making her videos, but didn't elaborate about them. Like an information sponge, she took everything in, while releasing very little. He was flattered, but an hour later he stopped and changed direction.

"I have really enjoyed our visit. I feel like I have a new friend; I hope it's mutual. We still haven't broached what *you* wanted to talk about. It seemed important to you. I'm going to shut up now, so I can hear what you have to say."

She heaved a deep sigh. "I don't want you to think I'm crazy, so I've been putting this off. Years ago, I started having dreams. The dreams were all different – at least, I think they were. I don't remember many details, but they all had the same man in them.

"This wasn't occasional. *Every night* for the past three years I've had these dreams, with the same man in all of them! Details have slipped away, but the face I've seen in bed at night, every night for so long is burned into my memory. That's how I recognize you. You are the face in my dreams! I can't explain it; can you?"

"I don't know," he told her honestly. "Is there anything else you remember?"

"Yes, one thing stands out. After every dream, when I wake up, I'm... happy! I have forged my life to my liking. I thought I was content, fulfilled, if a bit lonely; but when I wake up from these dreams, I'm happier than I've ever been. I never realized how unhappy I was until I started dreaming about you, a man I only met today. Seeing you has rattled me to the core; I don't know what to do!"

Allen took her by the hand; it shook a little but clasped his tightly.

"Hey, it's okay," he said softly. "I don't understand all this, but I can tell you what I believe."

Her eyes were wet, her gaze locked on his face.

"I serve the God of the Bible and trust in the Lord Jesus Christ. For three years – three years! That's when my ex-wife left! Wow! For three years, the Lord prepared you to recognize me when He planned for our paths to cross today. He apparently determined we should meet. I'm glad He did, because I've been feeling empty since I lost my best friend. Can we stay in touch? I'd really like us to keep talking, if that's okay with you."

A couple of tears ran down her cheeks, but her eyes lit up. She nodded with gusto, then they exchanged phone numbers.

CHAPTER 2

“ “I don't know for sure, but if I've come to the right conclusions, I expect you won't be dreaming about me anymore. The dreams may have served their purpose.”

She sat back in the driver's seat, pulling her hand away. He felt a twinge of regret at that; he liked holding her hand. Her eyes were locked on his when she spoke.

“God, huh? I've always been like the ultimate realist. If something doesn't affect me and can't be seen, it doesn't warrant my time or attention. I've occasionally had the feeling someone was watching what I was doing, but when I looked around and didn't see anyone, I put it out of mind.

“For most of my life, I would have blown off anyone trying to tell me about God, but the last three years have given me reason to reconsider. Post-menopausal effects like hot flashes don't begin to explain a recurring dream with a stranger's face that I finally meet in a public place.”

"Aren't you kind of young to have gone through menopause?" he asked, immediately thinking he shouldn't have said that. It was too personal.

"Really?" With a wicked smile she set the trap. "How old do you think I am?"

"Me and my big mouth. I am so burned!"

"Maybe not," the smile broadened to a wide grin that lit up her face, "depending on your answer. Be honest, now."

Taking a deep breath, he said, "Forty-six?"

"Nicely done," she laughed. "No doghouse for you. I'm fifty-four."

"No way! You're only two years younger than I am? How can you look so fantastic – I mean, how," he stumbled into silence and turned beet red, acutely aware how he had revealed his attraction to her.

"So that's how you look speechless, hmm?" She leaned forward, taking his hot red face in her hands, then pulling him to within a couple of inches of her own. "It's a good look for you." She leaned forward to kiss him, a quick brushing of lips followed by a tender wet lingering caress. Tongue-tied, he thought he saw sincere affection mingled with obvious amusement on her face as she sat back.

"I take care of myself. I'm an athlete in the course of my work, which is competitive in the extreme." Seeing his puzzlement, she added, "We'll get back to that. My body is always in training: diet, exercise, a daily regimen. I'm aware I look 'fantastic', but like every woman, I never tire of hearing it. I'm thrilled you think so, especially since you've only seen me in this parka, which doesn't show me to my best advantage. Thank you for the compliment!

"Back on topic, I have one major quibble with the Bible. I don't like that it labels women as the weaker sex. I find that stereotype very offensive."

"Where does it say that?" he asked.

"I don't know, exactly. I haven't got a lot of familiarity with it, but everyone knows about that part in my circles. I think it might be in the New Testament, what I've heard of it."

"Could it be the instruction, 'Husbands, give honor to your wives as the weaker vessels'?"

"*Yes*, that's it, I think. That calls women weak and claims men are stronger. I have proven for years that if anything, the opposite is true."

She had some strong opinions in this area. He wondered if he might be about to step into a minefield. "Why is there so much prevailing opinion in the world that men are stronger than women?" he ventured. "Could it be because we are generally bigger?"

She thought about it, finally admitting, "Probably."

He went on, "A size advantage isn't the only edge one person can have over another, but it is the most plainly visible. Whether male or female, the person having the advantage can be tempted to bully the more vulnerable person. Is it right to give in to the temptation?"

"Of course not!" Her reply was emphatic.

"That's what the scripture is about, bullying. We are to bear up our more vulnerable spouse, who should feel safe in our presence and not flinch when we reach for them. Women are definitely capable of bullying, too, and it's just as wrong for an abusive woman as it is for a man. Paul addressed men because their size and more aggressive tendencies usually ended up with them being the abusers."

She mulled that over, "So it's about abuse, not about superiority."

"Exactly. Another verse says, 'Husbands, love your wives, as Christ loved the church and gave Himself for it.' Sacrificing one's self for another is the highest form of love. Superiority doesn't figure into that. Spousal abuse is the opposite of love. The stronger partner bears responsibility to temper his or her strength with an extra helping of tenderness for the mate, so that partner will feel safe."

"That's beautiful! It also makes sense." A moment passed before she spoke again. "I've got to tell you what I do. If you want to leave and lose my number after you hear it, I won't bother you further. You and I live in different cultures. Sometimes different cultures don't mix; but you've been open with me about yourself, so I want to be the same with you. Have you heard of session wrestling?"

"Isn't that where men with more money than they need and not too much sense pay athletic young ladies to prove they can hurt them?"

She roared with laughter. He couldn't help but smile as he waited for her to recover. With an effort, she gathered her composure.

"Oh, that's hilarious! Right on the money, too, but I won't be offering you work promoting my company. There's such a thing as too much honesty in advertising!" She laughed some more. "I've got to tell Stefanie what you said. She's my business partner. I'll catch her while she's eating and has a mouthful of food. She will blow chunks!"

"That's kind of ornery," he stated mildly.

"Ornery! I like that! Yes, it is, but it will sure be fun!" He waited for her to continue.

"We employ a stable of lady grapplers that *bully* men who are willing to pay for the experience. We dress according to their request and, as you said, prove we can hurt them for as long a time period as they can afford, or until they've had all they can stand. It's not cheap for them, but we make decent bank for our sweat and effort. It sounds like it goes against what you just explained to me, but our customers pay for that treatment, so we give them their money's worth!"

"You do this, too? No offense, but you just don't look that intimidating."

The crooked wolfish smile appeared once more. "That's part of the mystique. The more demure the lady appears, the more shocked the guys are when they have to tap out! It adds to the humiliation when the woman that breaks your will is smaller and doesn't seem to be a threat.

"I've been doing this for decades. I've broken countless men, made them tap out, knocked them out, even made them cry like babies. Sometimes I've done all three to the same guy!

"I'm much stronger than I look. I have educated myself in anatomy and leverage to cause maximum pain with minimal effort. It's not just my opinion, but an industry consensus that I am one of the best wrestlers in the world today. It's not bragging, when you can back up what you claim!"

"So, I'm sitting next to a woman that can break me into pieces without working up a sweat. I'm a bit intimidated now," he admitted.

"You believe me? Without wanting proof?"

"Why would you lie to me? I'm nobody."

She seemed stunned. Leaning toward him, she laid her hand on his forearm. "You are unlike anyone I have ever met, the invader of my dreams. I'll let you in on a secret. When I'm around a guy any length of time, my mind begins to develop a tactical strategy to put him at my mercy. It just works that way, like a warrior mentality. I can't help how I think, even though I don't act on it.

"Usually, I would have a strategy in mind to put a man sitting where you are at a total loss of mobility and render him defenseless. *The thought of hurting you upsets my stomach!* If you were to raise a hand to me, I could defend myself, don't get me wrong; however, it would all be reaction. I have no preset strategy for you."

Those lovely blue eyes never left his.

"That should worry me, but it doesn't. The man in my dreams wouldn't hurt a fly. I know him to be gentle, kind and trustworthy to a fault. That's why I am so at ease with you."

He sat up straight, "Then your dreams aren't completely accurate." She tilted her head quizzically. "I'd kill a fly, especially if it annoyed me," he deadpanned. It was good for a chuckle.

"No, the scripture we discussed doesn't apply to your livelihood. What you have with your customers isn't a relationship built on trust. It's a transaction for services rendered laid out in a legal agreement, I expect."

She nodded.

"I thought so, to spell out obligations and limit liabilities. If someone is goofy enough to lay out money to get beat up, then the bruises only serve as proof of purchase. That's nothing like spousal abuse. Your clientele can go home and lick their wounds. Domestic abuse takes place in the home, leaving the victims without a place of their own to hide.

"I can't pass a moral judgment on what you do, either. *I* wouldn't be comfortable doing it, just as I wouldn't be comfortable working for a beer distributor, bar tending or taking bets for a casino. It's just as well, since I don't have the feminine allure your customers expect to encounter." That brought a smile.

"Anyway, without training, I'd be the one getting beat. No, I'll be keeping your number. You're not getting rid of me that easily."

CHAPTER 3

They continued to visit until his cell rang at 11:20 a.m. It was Ruth, his mom. Having noticed he wasn't home yet, she was beginning to worry. He told her he was fine, that he had stopped off to eat and was visiting with a new friend. An idea struck him. He asked her to hold on for a minute, then covered the mouthpiece.

"Mom's up," he said.

"Yeah, I heard. Do you need to leave?"

"Not for her; she's okay, just got worried when she saw I wasn't home yet. I do need to take a shot, though." Her puzzled expression prompted more information, "I'm diabetic."

Puzzlement turned to concern. "Did I keep you from…"

Allen cut her off, "I'm fine, my sugar is under control. Since she's up... I don't know if you have time... would you follow me home to meet her?"

She barely hesitated. "I'd love to."

"Hey, Mom, do you feel up to meeting my new friend if she comes home with me?"

"She?" He could sense her shock. "Uh, yeah. I'll get ready." She sounded dazed.

"Okay, Ma. Be there in about 15 minutes."

"See you soon."

On the way home, his mind fluttered over Erin; the miraculous way they met, the things she had told him about herself, and the way he had poured himself out to her. That last was no surprise. His tendency was to be too open with people. He never learned how to guard his heart.

He chided himself for talking too much. Well, what's done is done. He hoped it wouldn't cost him. Close friends didn't come easy for Allen. Losing this one would be disappointing. He wanted Ruth's impression of her, not trusting his own ability to be objective. He was thrilled Erin agreed to meet her and hoped they would get on well.

When they arrived, Erin asked about the old gray Buick sitting in the driveway. He explained it belonged to his son, who had recently moved out to live with his girlfriend. They were expecting twins. The car needed some work to be driveable, but he couldn't afford the repairs. When asked if they had a cost estimate, he cited about $600.

She asked his name and he replied, "Anthony." The name seemed meaningful to her, though she didn't say why. She wanted to know if he had transportation. Allen had loaned him his own car, since he was using Ruth's van.

He added, "She rarely drives anymore. I take her most places she needs to go."

They went in, where he introduced his mom. She told Erin to call her Ruth. At his request, Erin described her dreams, leading up to how they met. Ruth agreed that the dreams must have served their purpose, since no other explanation made sense.

From then on, the two of them visited nonstop; he just listened. Erin called her "Miss Ruth" at one point. She tried to correct her, but Erin said it felt disrespectful to her and asked if 'Miss Ruth' was okay. She acceded, shaking her head.

Remembering he still needed to take a shot and morning meds, he excused himself. When he returned, his mother asked him to get her cell phone. He retrieved it from her bedroom, then was directed to give it to Erin so she could enter her number.

Erin filled him in as she worked, "In case something unexpected happens to you, I asked your mom to notify me and she said she would. You never know when an emergency might come up." As she gave the cell back to her, she hesitated a moment, then squatted down next to her chair.

"Miss Ruth, I can't tell you how glad I am that we met. You've come to mean a lot to me in less time than your son did, and that's saying something. If you ever need anything – and I do mean *anything* – please let me know."

They had gotten on well, but he had no idea she made such an impression. Ruth seemed taken aback as well. She said thanks a lot, but she could still do most things herself and Allen took good care of her. Erin said she was sure of that, but everyone needs help sometimes. She asked if it would be alright to call her to visit. Ruth said sure, then stood to hug her, saying it was very nice meeting her and how pleased she was that Allen had a new friend.

He walked Erin back to her car. She hadn't left, yet he was already missing her! She started the car, then leaned over to do something in the passenger seat that he couldn't see. With her leg still dangling out, he waited to close the door.

After a moment she stepped back out, handing him a check. It was written out to Anthony for $1,000! "To help him get his car fixed," she briefed him.

"H-how am I supposed to explain this?" he was floored.

She chuckled, "Why not tell him the truth? Tell him your girlfriend wants to help him get his car repaired."

"G-g-g..." he stammered.

She put a finger on his lips with a grin, "When you find your voice, can you say that to him?"

He blushed, nodding wordlessly.

She added, "I know that's more than you quoted, but with babies on the way, no doubt he can put the rest to good use. Oh, for the record, this is a gift, not a loan, so don't attempt to repay me."

Her eyes full of mischief, she grinned again, "I love rendering you speechless! Do you think you can manage a goodbye kiss, in lieu of the words that are failing you?"

He could and did. Gathering her in his arms, he kissed her passionately. The response was hungry, inviting, an acceptance in her embrace that he had not felt in at least a decade. It took his breath away; he didn't want to let her go.

When she pulled back, she gasped. "Whew! We absolutely *must* pick this up where we left off when I come back in a few days. Will you call me tomorrow?"

He nodded.

She giggled, "If you have your voice back, that is. Hope your speechlessness isn't permanent." She got in the car. He closed the door, then she rolled the window down and he leaned forward.

"It isn't, I hope?"

Opening his mouth, he croaked, "Not sure."

Reaching behind him, she pulled his head to her and delivered another warm wet kiss, then she was gone.

CHAPTER 4

Allen had no idea how their encounter had skewed her travel plans. She decided hours ago that she would know what her dreams becoming reality meant before continuing on her way, despite the fact that she must be in Chicago by morning. She booked the first available flight using her cell phone, then called Stefanie en route to the airport.

Accommodations for the company had been arranged in advance, but now that she was flying rather than driving, it would be nice to have a familiar face waiting to take her to the hotel. Besides, she wanted to tell Stef what happened. Erin was boiling over with the news.

Stefanie was more than a business partner; she was her best friend and confidant. Forty-one years old, everything about Stef was solid; from her practical way of thinking to her rock-hard bodybuilder physique, nothing seemed to shake her up. She was the only person Erin had told about her recurring dreams, before today.

Stefanie reassured Erin she was not cracking up, that people are not responsible for what their minds do when they sleep. She had no idea why Erin was dreaming the way she was, but what did it matter? Dreams are just dreams. You wake up and they are gone, so push aside the memory and get on with life. If Stef lacked anything, it was imagination. She did seem to understand how the dreams bothered Erin, so she listened patiently when Erin needed to talk.

Erin suspected they fascinated Stefanie as well, over time. She formed that impression when Stef started asking about details of each night's visions before Erin spoke of them, a few weeks after they began. Her partner was curious, despite her apparent nonchalance.

When Stef answered her call, Erin told her she had a change of plan. She would be arriving at O'Hare Airport at 10:20 p.m. Stef said she would have someone there to pick her up and asked if everything was okay.

"Better than okay," Erin told her. "I have news you won't believe. It's the man in my dreams; I met him today!" Dead silence answered her for long enough that she finally said, "Hello?"

Stefanie's voice had an odd sound to it when she spoke again, like she was a long way from the phone. "He looked like the man in your dreams?"

"He didn't just resemble him, Stef – it *was* him!"

Another silence, then "*I* will pick you up myself. I want to hear everything. Have you checked in and got your ticket? Never mind, I will wait until you get here. Did he act like the man in the dreams? Of course he did, or you wouldn't be so excited. This is too weird! The dreams were weird, but now they are real? You're right, I don't believe it! But you never lie to me! You are serious, right? You do not pull off my leg?"

Stef was a Bulgarian immigrant who took pride in her American citizenship. She worked painstakingly at losing her thick East European accent, usually sounding like she was born here; but sometimes, her off-kilter rendering of colloquialisms still gave her away. Erin smiled at the slip, being careful not to laugh out loud.

"No, I'm not pulling your leg. I'm at the airport. I have to hang up now, but I'll tell you everything when I see you, okay?"

She heard faint grumbling she could not make out. It sounded like Stef had lapsed into her native tongue, something she did on rare instances when she was exasperated. Between that and the rambling, it was obvious that her friend was completely beside herself!

"And Stef," she added, noting that the grumbling stopped, "we talked for hours. As far as I can tell, he is *exactly* like in the dreams."

"Gahh! Now you are teasing me! Get here so we can talk!" Stef hung up.

CHAPTER 5

"So, what do you think, Mom?" Having showed her the check written out to her grandson and told her how Erin identified as his girlfriend, Allen wanted her more objective point of view. He felt like a tornado had tossed him high into the air; he was struggling to regain his footing.

"I like her. She's obviously not a Christian, but there is nothing phony about her that I could see. Beneath her tough facade, she seems to be a sweet girl with a tender heart. What do you think of her?"

"She scares me, or maybe it's my reaction to her that scares me, I'm not sure which. I could fall for her so easily; I'm afraid I already am! After the divorce, I had no intention of ever getting involved with a woman again. I don't know if that's hurt talking, or fear of being hurt again, or selling myself short.

"I'm not a young man anymore. A relationship is so much work that the adventure just doesn't appeal to me.

The idea doesn't appeal, but Erin...!" Ruth listened quietly, waiting while he searched for words.

"She's smart, she's beautiful and she listens to me. She wants to hear what I have to say. Most people don't, they just want to have their say and tune you out, you know? She doesn't come across as humoring me; she seems really interested in me.

"I am such a sucker for a girl that pays attention to me! Add to that the fact that she is completely out of my league; gorgeous, successful, more self-confident than I ever dreamt of being! It makes for a mismatch of epic proportions," he finished and went quiet.

"The Lord doesn't seem to think so," Ruth said. "He's been planning this for a long time, remember? Ever since you were abandoned, He's been working to bring Erin into your life. He knows what you need better than you do, so don't sell Him short."

She let that sink in before continuing, "She looks at you the way I used to look at your dad. Are you aware that she loves you?"

He looked up sharply. "How could she? We just met!"

"No," she told me, "you just met her. She's been seeing you every night for the last three years. It's not a case of love at first sight; she loves the man she's been seeing. God put a love for you in her heart before you two met in real life."

His head swam at the thought. The Lord is kind to those who trust in Him, but this was beyond imagination!

"But the man in her dreams isn't real!" he objected.

"Isn't he? If God designed those dreams, don't you think He could portray you accurately? You said Erin is smart. If you fell short of the man she's come to know and love, she couldn't help but notice. In the time you two visited, she took your measure. Honey, she was not disappointed! That's how I know her dreams came from Him; only He could paint you so accurately to her.

"The Lord knows your heart. He knows how broken it feels right now. Of course, her soul is His chief concern, that she would be saved. We both know that's His top priority." He nodded agreement. "But if this was His only purpose in bringing her to you, that would be cruel to both of you. He doesn't work like that."

Taking a breath, she went on, "Remember what God said of Adam in Genesis? 'It is not good that man should be alone.' He decided to make him a helper comparable to him, so He formed Eve for that role. He started matchmaking then! Since He doesn't change, He never stopped. This is His doing, son.

"But don't take my word for it, see how it plays out. She lives more than a thousand miles from you. We both know how difficult long-distance relationships are. You can't afford to go see her and she knows it. If she wants to explore what she has labeled a romance by calling herself your girlfriend, the ball is entirely in her court. Let's see what she does with it."

Now that made sense. "At least I can call her," he said.

Ruth smiled. "You should, and often. Make sure she knows her interest in you is reciprocated. In this relationship, she is the initiator, and you are the respondent, which is not the way most relationships work. For you two, however, this is the only way it *could* work. She has such a strong personality that the role will come easy for her, while you are broken to the point that you don't have the heart to pursue anyone.

"If the Lord has put sufficient love in her heart for you, nothing will keep her from you. All you need to do is decide whether or not to accept her love."

CHAPTER 6

When Stefanie picked Erin up at the airport, they went to the hotel, brought in her luggage and ordered room service. By this time, Erin reflected on her friend's reaction to the news to reach a surprising conclusion. Stef wasn't just interested in her dreams turned reality; she was emotionally invested in them! She didn't think their friendship alone was sufficient to explain it. Something about Stef herself had sucked her into the mystery.

It made her curious, but she sidelined her questions while she brought her friend up to date on the day's events. Stefanie stood by her when she took her into her confidence, gave her the moral support she needed when the dreams caused her to question her sanity. She deserved to know the outcome before Erin raised queries Stef might consider too personal.

So Erin told her everything. This time, Stefanie was the information sponge. She soaked it all in until Erin finished, then went back to ask for clarifications about specific details. Stef had always been an attentive listener with the kind of memory Erin secretly envied. Though it was Erin who experienced all those dreams, she suspected Stef retained more of their content from their countless discussions than Erin could remember, as her recollections faded over time.

"He said the dreams came from God? And you *listened*?" Stef inquired. The second question had the emphasis; she knew Erin had little patience for what she considered nonsense.

"Yes, I did!" Erin was a bit defensive. "I've seen this man's face for years in my dreams, then he steps out in front of me in real life. He could have told me Santa Claus is real; I might not have believed him, but I would have listened to his reasoning at this point! Besides, it at least gives us some theory for where the dreams originate. That's more than we ever came up with."

"True," Stef allowed. Stefanie could portray convincing facial expressions in an instant. Her lower lip began to quiver and her eyes welled up with tears as she took on the appearance of a lost waif. Before she could think, Erin wondered what had so disturbed her friend. Stef choked out in a forlorn little girl's voice, "Wh-What do y-you mean, S-Santa's not real?" then broke into a huge grin.

Both of them laughed. Stef had a knack for disarming tense situations with her talents that Erin admired, even when she felt taken in. "Guess we should let you get to bed so you can test his theory, hmm?" She started to get up to go to her own room.

"Hang on, would you?" Erin stopped her. "What do you think of this?"

"Which part?" Stef wanted to know.

"All of it!" Erin was exasperated. "That a figment of my imagination has turned out to be a real person! That he actually seems to be like this imaginary man! That can't be faked, unless he saw my dreams to copy them – and that's ridiculous! But *God* led me to a total stranger I am more comfortable with than I am in my own skin? That is ridiculous and crazy!

"Is God real? And the worst of it is – Stef, *I want the dream*! I've always wanted it, but it wasn't real until today! Is it possible I might have it? To dare believe it might be attainable?"

Stef settled back in, pondering a moment before responding. "Erin, have you wondered why all this matters to me, besides that it was happening to you and you matter to me?"

"Actually, yes, I have, especially after our talk on the phone earlier. I had no idea you were so invested in these mysterious dreams. Nothing I said was meant to tease you, really! I'm sorry if it felt that way."

"No problem. I embarrassed myself with that outburst. I try to keep my feelings to myself, but your news was like a bomb going off. I guess I should have expected such a bombshell sooner or later."

"We've never discussed our beliefs because you weren't open to the subject. You were stuck on the material world. That only began to change when you couldn't escape your recurring dreams. Something intangible had a grip on you that knocked you completely out of your comfort zone."

Erin nodded silently. Stefanie had never opened up like this before; she thought it might be costing her, which Erin valued even more. She needed her friend's candidness.

"I *know* there are intangibles that affect our lives. Moreover, they are not random; there is intelligence in their timing and how they affect us, sometimes beneficially, sometimes malevolent. You are like my older sister; I look up to you. The dreams were something special that I became convinced would somehow shape the direction of your life. I think they are good, since you wake up happy.

"I believe we all have a kind of grand adventure at least once. We come to face life's greatest questions with an opportunity to find the answers that matter most to us. I think this is *your* adventure. I am hoping some of the answers you find will spill over onto me. Does that make sense?"

"Yes, I suppose it does," Erin replied. "I've been so embroiled in the midst of this thing that I never gave any thought to how it might affect you. You were my sounding board, confidant and advisor. It just didn't occur how you might be impacted by what I was experiencing. I'm so so-"

"Don't you dare apologize to me!" Stef declared, cutting her off. "I feel privileged that you let me into your personal world. It was never my intent to make you regret it!"

Erin leaned forward, taking her hand. "I don't regret it at all, Stef. You are more than my business partner. You are my best friend; that's the truth!"

"That's true now, but it is changing. I think you will share your life with Allen in a way you and I never could. I don't begrudge that; I'm actually excited for you."

She started to object, but Stefanie held up her hand, "You asked me what I think, so I am giving you what *you* requested." It was true, so Erin went silent.

"Erin, I think you are strong enough to have whatever you want, once you determine what that is, including your dreams. If it's a man, he doesn't stand a chance of resisting you! But even you cannot dream a man into existence, sister. You asked me if God is real. If those dreams have turned out to be real, they certainly have a real source, so I think you have your answer.

"But it raises more questions. Why does your happiness matter to God? If it does, why did He wait until so late in your life to get your attention? Or maybe it is not you that is important to Him. Allen believes in Him, so perhaps he is the one being favored, and you are lucky to be chosen to share in the blessing meant for him.

"I do not share Allen's belief, but I am jealous of how sure he is in his acceptance of the Bible. Since he cleared up that 'weaker sex' nonsense as a misunderstanding, I think I will look into it. Maybe even if you dream of him again, *if* you ever go to bed and sleep!" she ended with a wink.

Erin smiled and nodded, getting up slowly. Stef had impeccable logic. It was a lot to think about. She hugged Stef, thanking her for her insight before she left. With a strange sense of peace, she went to bed and fell asleep immediately.

CHAPTER 7

Allen had difficulty resting through the night. His mind was overly active with the day's events, but working overnights messed with his sleep schedule on nights off, anyway. He napped for three hours after Erin left in the afternoon, then didn't get sleepy until after 3:30 a.m. He got around for the day about 9:00 a.m. Monday. Ruth wasn't up yet, so he ate breakfast before calling Erin a bit after 10.

"Hi, you!" she greeted him cheerfully.

"Good morning! You sound chipper today. Are you on the road?"

"Huh? Oh, no, I flew in last night and left my car in Springfield. I had to be here this morning."

"Ouch! I didn't know that. Guess I messed up your plans."

"No, I chose to revise them after meeting you; that was in no way your fault. I don't regret a thing, so don't you go there, either. Capisce?"

"Got it. How are you? Did you manage to get any rest?"

"Some," she replied. "I wouldn't mind some more, but I'll be okay. Seems you were right; for the first time in three years, I didn't dream. I kind of missed that moment of euphoria upon waking, though. I got used to that."

"Well, maybe you will get used to hearing my voice in your ear when you are awake, instead. I plan to call you at least once every day and make a pest of myself. The sound of your voice is something I'd rather not deprive myself of."

"Listen to this!" she laughed. "Not only has he got his voice back, he's become a sweet talker! That's what I call a full recovery. Truthfully, the sound of your voice more than makes up for the loss the dream. Thanks for calling. How did you rest?"

"About like normal. Being a day sleeper makes it awkward on days off, when you try to stay up because everyone else is up. Funny thing, though; the night you stopped dreaming of me, I dreamt of you."

"*Yes*! It's about time it happens to you instead of me! Don't leave out any details! You do remember it, don't you?"

"Vividly. In my dream, I was standing outside. You stood about twenty feet away, dressed in the parka and ski pants you wore yesterday, though it was sunny. As you walked toward me, I noticed that even in the parka you were shivering. You came up to me, then turned around. I removed your coat and laid it aside, putting my arms around you as you leaned back into me.

"You put your arms over mine as I held you. The shivering subsided, then stopped. You relaxed back into my embrace, turned your head to look over your shoulder and said, 'It's *so good* to be home.' That was the end of it."

Silence answered him, then an odd choking sound. "Erin?" he asked.

A little higher pitched than usual, she said, "I'll call you back," and hung up. He wondered if he said something wrong, then remembered she was working. There was no telling what might have needed her immediate attention, so he let it go and settled in to wait for her call.

In the boxing gym she rented, Erin had access to a small office. She was standing near the door while on the phone and quickly ducked in when she hung up. No one noticed her go in, but eagle-eyed Stefanie saw the light go on and got a glimpse of Erin with tears on her cheeks as she was closing the blinds in the single window. She spoke with Pam (one of their senior staff), giving her instructions to keep things moving, then followed Erin into the little office.

She found her in the chair behind the desk with her head in her hands, sobbing so hard she was shaking. She went around the desk, leaned over and tried to put her arms around Erin's shoulders; but she turned, rose and hugged her tightly in a full embrace. Feeling awkward, Stef wrapped her arms around her while she cried, wondering what had upset her.

The Metal Lady, as the women of the company had dubbed her, was always a picture of iron composure. None of them, Stef included, had ever known Erin to fall apart like this. At a loss, she held her close, waiting for her to collect herself. It didn't take long. After a couple of minutes, Erin stepped back and wiped her tears, her normally pale face a hot red. She took a tissue off the desk to blow her nose, then sat down again, waving Stef to another seat. Fixing her gaze on her, she began to speak.

"Thanks; that was just what I needed, a shoulder to cry on. I'm sorry about behaving like that, and more than a little embarrassed." She went on to describe Allen's dream. Stefanie didn't interrupt, but personally she heard nothing that could explain Erin's response. It sounded nice to her.

Erin continued, "You may have noticed I avoid speaking about my past, particularly my childhood." Stef nodded. "That's because I don't like to recall it. I was abandoned at an early age. I grew up as an orphan in foster care. The first home the state placed me in was not a good place, so I ran away. I never bonded with any of those families, which was largely my fault, as I acted out a lot. That's why it means so much when you consider me as your big sister; you are the closest thing I have to a family.

"And without a family, I have never had a home. Owning a house is just laying claim to real estate. Home is where someone is waiting for you, happy to see you when you arrive. Allen, like you, didn't know any of this when he told me of his dream; but it hit me like a forty-car freight train when he said I relaxed into his arms and told him how good it was to be *home*."

Stef's eyes were watering. "I had no idea. But I meant what I said – you *are* my sister. That will never change, no matter what happens." She hesitated a moment. "You know where the dreams came from now, since they stopped last night. Three years to prepare you for Allen, one night to prepare Allen for you. Guess that shows which of you is more hardheaded," she laughed.

Erin couldn't help laughing. She needed that lift. If this God Allen spoke of had taken notice of her (and the evidence was piling up), then it wasn't just for the last three years. He had full knowledge of her life from the time she was little; furthermore, He knew exactly how to get to her. It would be terrifying, except that He seemed to have her best interests in mind.

She needed to find out more, fast! The fastest way she could think of was to ask Allen what he thought God might want from her. Talking to Allen was something she looked forward to, anyway; besides, she did promise to call back. Why wait?

CHAPTER 8

"Well, hello! Is everything okay now?" Allen said, answering Erin's call.

"It's better."

"What happened? It wasn't something I said, was it?" Something in the sound of her voice suggested that she had been crying.

"No, it wasn't you. It was... your dream." She hesitated, then said petulantly, "Your God doesn't play fair! My dreams shook me for years. When you have one, it should rock your world, not mine, not again!"

"I don't understand, Erin, but I can tell you this; He rocked my world yesterday when He brought you into it! Does that make you feel any better?"

She giggled in spite of herself. "Actually, yes it does, a little. It's sweet of you to say, and you're going to get kissed when I see you next!"

She told him about her past, why his dream impacted her so powerfully. He said he had no clue it would carry such meaning. She was quick to admit she knew that, so she didn't hold him responsible. She joked that he was not to dream about her anymore, that her heart was not up to more such shocks! He reminded her that just as she couldn't control her dreams, he had no control over his. He offered to keep future dreams to himself. She warned him he better not!

Erin became serious. "Allen, this is scary. Some God I don't know teaches me in my dreams to recognize you, a total stranger, when I see you. He arranges for us to meet three years in advance, at least. I am grateful for this; it's like we are soulmates finally getting acquainted, something long overdue. But He seems to know things about me I've tried hard to forget! Nothing in life is free. What does He want from me?"

"He wants fellowship, Erin. He wants you to know Him, to know how much He loves you. He wants you to see how He has always been with you to bring you to the place in life where you are now.

"When you wrestle someone, you take note of their weaknesses so you can exploit them to win the match, don't you? Well, God watches as we wrestle with the issues of life so He can uphold us in our weaknesses, to keep us from being destroyed.

"Once you accept that He is real, you face another reality that is not so pleasant – the devil. Scripture says his intent is to kill, steal and destroy. Like your opponent, he wants to take advantage of your vulnerabilities; but unlike an opponent on the mats, he doesn't consider the match won until he inflicts a mortal wound! *He* really doesn't play fair, but God helps by keeping his cheating tactics in check."

"Like a referee," Erin said.

"Yes, but He is better by far. Every wrestler is stuck with a fatal disadvantage – we eventually tire. When we are exhausted and defenseless, our immortal enemy is still coming at us. The outcome is certain, unless we surrender to Jesus Christ first. He is the only person ever to defeat the devil decisively! If we ask Him into our hearts and to forgive our sins, He stands between us and our tireless adversary. Satan knows he cannot get past Jesus to destroy us, unless he can lure us out from under His protection."

"You don't sound like you are reciting a creed or a belief system," Erin observed. "I mean, you don't sound like you're trying to be convincing. You sound convinced of what you're telling me."

"Would you respect me if I wasn't? You told me how you ladies break a man's will by inflicting pain until he submits. If we competed, you could probably break me; but that's just it, I'm already broken! I have failed before, more times than I can count. My marriage was only my most recent failure. My ego is small, because I know that as I have failed in life before, it's likely I'll fail again at something I consider important."

She was incredulous. "That's so depressing! How do you live with so much despair?"

He chuckled, "I don't despair. My confidence isn't in my success; it's in Christ's. My failures are not decisive, so long as He puts me back on my feet and gets me going again.

"There is a verse in the book of Micah that says, 'Do not rejoice over me, my enemy; when I fall, I will arise; when I sit in darkness, the Lord shall be a light unto me.' No matter how many times I am knocked down hard, I'm not defeated until I choose to stay down."

"I've had a few opponents like that. The only way to stop them is to knock them out, when they utterly refuse to submit; but a KO just provides time to exit the fight. If I stuck around, I know that when they wake up, they will get up, ready for more. They are unbreakable, the reason we set time limits on matches. But wouldn't it be better to *win*?"

"The world celebrates winners for a while, then it goes into the record books and is forgotten. The Lord celebrates overcomers, upholding us until our fight is over, then receiving us proudly afterward. Winning relies on ability and maybe some luck; either you have it, or you don't. All you can do is train to increase your chances. 'Never say die' is a choice, an attitude based on commitment. Age, illness or an opponent that outclasses you will not stop you if you are determined to keep trying.

"It's like you, Erin. You are way out of my league, yet you are talking to me now. How do I deserve you? I don't! Yet you care about me. I've done nothing to earn your affection. I am in *awe* that God has done this for me. I am waiting for you to wake up and realize you could do so much better than me, and I'm thrilled it hasn't happened yet!

"At the risk of sounding selfish, I hope it never does. If your heart is won over to me, it wasn't my doing. He has won it for me with your approval, and I am overwhelmed with the grace both of you are showing me!"

He was in tears at this point, completely out of words. There was silence on the line for a couple of minutes while he tried to and finally did dry up. Some sniffing proved she was still there.

She came back, "How do you expect us to talk if you keep making me cry?" They both laughed. "I'm not a spring chicken, Allen. Remember? Nor am I a virgin. I know what kind of men are out there, or at least I thought I did until I met you. If I wanted one of them, I could have my pick.

"I am not sleepwalking. I am wide awake. God revealed you to me before I knew you existed, but I choose you! I choose you because I want you. There is no way I am letting you go, short of you deciding to run for your life! And if you want to run, you better start now, because I know where you live!"

She laughed again, the most beautiful sound he ever heard. He couldn't help joining in.

"I guess I got told," he said.

"Yes, you did. I hope I don't have to repeat myself, mister."

"No, ma'am. You came through loud and clear. I won't go there again."

"Good! Nothing is more annoying than a hardheaded man who refuses to learn his lesson." She chuckled, "Though according to Stefanie, my having dreams for three years as opposed to your one night indicates that I am more hardheaded than you!"

That cracked him up all over again. They laughed and shared some more before saying goodbye.

They spoke daily after that. Sometimes the conversations lasted longer, sometimes shorter, but they were the highlight of his day. Very rarely, she was too busy to talk, promising to call him back. She never failed to keep her promise. He began to realize how much she meant to him. He said he could fall for her, and he did. He thought he might have the day he met her; whatever the case, there remained no doubt now!

When he told Ruth how he felt, her response surprised him. "Good! Honey, you're not good alone. You need a partner you can trust; one person who will love, respect and believe in you, no matter what. God chose this girl, putting her hand in yours for both your sakes.

"In some ways, you are so insightful, but in some things you are very naïve. God has protected you all your life; even when your marriage wasn't good, it provided a hedge of protection around you. You are too vulnerable; you are clueless how a cruel and ruthless woman could utterly destroy you. Believe me, there are some out there! I've been praying for you, and am convinced that His answer is Erin. If I don't live to see the rapture of the church, I believe you will be in good hands."

"Thanks, Mom. That means a lot. But stick around, will you? It's really nice having you here." He hugged her.

"Thanks, but you know that's not up to me. I really do miss your dad."

"I know, Mom. I miss him, too." His parents had been together 47 years; he could only imagine her loneliness. He hoped she understood that she was as much a comfort to him as he tried to be for her.

CHAPTER 9

Erin returned the following weekend. He offered her the guest room in advance, but she declined for a motel, saying she could make use of the weight room and pool. It reminded him how her lifestyle was so different from his, not to mention what she could afford. Her world was very different than his; love seemed to be the only thing connecting them. He wondered if it might be enough.

She arrived Saturday afternoon, the day before his weekend began. He offered to pick her up at the airport, but she reminded him her car was there. When she arrived, he met her with a huge hug and a kiss. She laughingly kissed him again. "I told you I had one reserved for you, Sweet Talker." He declared how he had missed her, and she said the same.

Ruth asked about her trip and wanted to know if she was hungry. Erin said she wasn't, but would be in a couple of hours. In the meanwhile, she hoped he would go with her to check into the motel and help bring in her luggage. She planned to go home Wednesday morning after breakfast. Ruth inquired if they had dinner plans. Erin said yes before he could respond.

"I guess we do, Mom."

"I'm sorry," Erin backtracked, "but I have been looking forward to this all week. Do you mind if I kidnap your son before he has to go to work?"

She laughed, "I can understand that. You two have fun."

They left in Erin's car to get her checked into the motel. After the luggage was in, he admired how nice the room was, but Erin took it for granted. She had stayed in so many over the years that they had ceased to impress her.

She stated that a number of companies she worked with before starting her own business filmed in motel rooms. He wondered how, when there isn't that much space? She explained that they would move the beds to make room, then put them back before they left.

Didn't the motels object? She said they might have, had they known what was happening. Once the rooms are rented, what people do in them is their own business, as long as it isn't illegal.

"You would be amazed what people use motel rooms to do, sometimes legal, sometimes not," she told him.

That made him curious. He began to ask questions, not sure if he would like the answers. "Erin, I don't know much about what you do. I don't mean to offend, but does wrestling lead to sex?"

She didn't bat an eye. "It's a valid question. My company doesn't do that, but some do. A growing percentage of the industry is becoming porn, flouting prostitution laws and taking their chances at getting fined or prosecuted. I don't need that hassle.

"Law enforcement has sometimes sent in ringers, I suspect; officers posing as customers looking for matches with the girls to see if they are offered something more. Most of what we do is semi-competitive, not full-out competitive matches. The guys don't fight back, they cooperate and let us place them in holds, then endure as long as they can while trying to escape. We prefer semi-competitive because there is much less chance of someone getting seriously injured.

"The skimpy clothing we wear is titillation, but the holds are *real* and debilitating. Once we have them locked in and begin to taunt them, investigators are quickly embarrassed! They tend to cut the session short. Only guys who are into the titillation and humiliation stick around for more pain. Our reputation would suffer if we didn't provide their money's worth!

"Many of our customers don't wrestle. They want to be entertained, often asking us to make a custom video of a specific tableau. If they agree to the price we quote, or if we think it will be popular enough to interest a sufficient number of prospective buyers to make it profitable, we'll create the scenario.

"For example, one that is popular is a girl in bed asleep, wearing lingerie, being surprised by a burglar. She jumps him, takes him down and squeezes him to a pulp with her legs. It's titillating, while the girl who would have been a victim has turned the tables on the bad guy, making it a fun clip.

"Videos like this have much more potential for profit than bruising a guy's ego in an individual session, along with selling videos of the sessions themselves. That's why I classify my business as video production, because that's where the money is!"

"What about nudity? Do you do that, with your company, I mean?"

"We don't do that, either, and it has cost us. We could increase our profits considerably by wrestling topless; we have estimated *tripling* our profit with that one step. I did it in my younger days, some. It seemed like no big deal at the time, but when I went online and saw how screenshots from those clips were multiplied across the web, I felt ashamed. I value the self-respect of my girls over whatever profit I might be giving up, so we stay in costume, even if it's just a string bikini.

She hesitated, "I have done some things in my life I'm not proud of; that was one of them. Do you think less of me now?"

"Erin, we all make mistakes. I'm not ashamed of you; I'm actually proud of you for trying to keep your girls from making the same mistake. I hope they appreciate how you are looking out for them!"

She beamed when he said he was proud of her. Kissing him gently, she said, "Thanks. That means a lot to me, especially coming from you. Let's go eat!"

They found a restaurant and continued to chat, devouring details about each other with an appetite that outstripped what they brought to the dinner table. There wasn't time for other activities to be planned after the meal, since he had to work, so they just relaxed and enjoyed visiting. Time went by quickly, so quickly! When the waiter brought the check, she immediately produced her bank card. He took it before her date could object.

Allen started as he walked away, "Erin, I-"

She put her index finger on his lips. "Look," she said, "I know about traditional values, how the guy likes to wine and dine his girl. It's a sweet notion. I have no intention of disrespecting you, but I also don't want my visits to be a burden. You and Miss Ruth make ends meet, but don't have much to spare, am I right?

"Allen, money is not a problem for me. Partially, that's due to hard work and careful investment, but a good part of it is due to the fact I had no one in my life to spend it upon. I would have traded my left arm for that special someone! Now that I have you, I have that opportunity. Please don't deny me the privilege!"

He sat back, deflated. "Erin, I can't argue with your logic, but I can't help but feel like I'm not carrying my weight. I'm not sure I can handle this."

She leaned over to take his chin in her hand. "We'll get through it, together. I can gladly cover our costs, because I'm not alone; and you can learn to benefit from generosity graciously, without letting it wound your pride, because you are not alone." She kissed him once, then twice. "Can we lean on each other in this?"

He took her hand, replied with a half-smile, "We can try."

She perked up instantly. "Good! Now let's go to McDonald's, so you can buy me an ice cream cone!"

He couldn't help but laugh, then that's just what they did before she took him home. He went to work thinking happy thoughts, looking forward to seeing her again tomorrow.

When Allen came home from work, he set his alarm for 2 p.m. so he wouldn't sleep all day. He woke to the alarm; en route to the bathroom, he heard voices. He finished his routine as fast as he could, wondering who was visiting. It turned out Ruth and Erin were sitting in the living room, talking.

Erin stood to hug him, then took his hand and led him back to sit with her on the couch. She explained that she had called to ask if she could visit while waiting for him to wake. Ruth said come on! She was making chicken and dumplings; the unique sound of the pressure cooker could be heard from the kitchen. The three of them continued getting acquainted into the afternoon and over a late lunch.

Allen had been wondering how Erin could just leave her business on a week's notice to have this extended weekend visit. He asked her about it, not knowing how to broach what he really wanted to know: how often would she be able to break free for more of them? Long distance relationships are tough for short periods, but they are well-nigh impossible for a long term. Erin clued them in about her circumstances and answered their questions, as Ruth said she had been wondering the same thing.

"I have been phasing myself into retirement slowly for almost as long as I was having the dreams about you, Allen. Stefanie runs the day to day operations of the company; she's very capable. I still help with some booking and I like to maintain my presence in training the girls, but I am becoming more of a silent partner. When the main draw of the business is titillation, pretty *young* girls are what viewers want to see, not someone old enough to be a grandmother.

"I've been hanging around them a lot more than I needed to be, but I honestly had nowhere else I wanted to go! Now you two have provided me that destination I never had before."

"So, you can come back whenever you want?" he asked, elated.

"For the most part, yes. As my own boss, technically I always could, but the demands of maintaining the business are not nearly what they used to be for me. I could have fully retired by now if I wanted, but retire to do what? Besides, Stef and the girls are the closest thing to family I have. They mean a lot to me. I like to think it's mutual. Sometimes I feel like a den mother!" she laughed.

"Well, you are more than welcome here anytime, Erin," Ruth declared. "We're very happy to have you. The guest room is yours whenever you are ready to use it."

"Thank you, Miss Ruth. I really appreciate that." She paused, looking thoughtful, then went on. "You know, I thought I had made all my dreams in life come true, until I came to this house. Allen, your son's name brought back one dream I had forgotten. I suppose it was the first dream

I had as a little girl! It reminded me that there were some happy times in my childhood, that it wasn't a total bust. Anthony: his name recalled Major Anthony Nelson to mind."

The other two smiled.

"As a little girl, I loved the TV show *I Dream of Jeannie*. I wanted to *be* Jeannie! Barbara Eden was so beautiful! Jeannie had power to do anything she wanted! She called him Master, but she had all the power. She didn't stay with him because he was truly her master, but because she was absolutely nuts about him!

"I wanted what she had; to be powerful enough to make good things happen, and to have a man that I would be totally crazy about!" Her eyes were watering. "I had forgotten all about that little girl's dream, yet after all these years it is coming true right before my eyes! Is that weird?"

"Not where the Lord is concerned," Ruth said. "He knows the innermost desires of our hearts, never forgetting a thing. He remembered your simple girlish dream, so He is showing you His love by giving it to you, something you never could have brought about on your own. He loves you, Erin," she ended quietly, "and we do, too."

Allen added, "For me, that goes double." Raising his hand to her cheek, he turned her face gently, until those entrancing blue eyes were locked on his. "I love you with all my heart, Erin Adams."

She broke. Throwing her arms around his neck, she sobbed and declared her love for him. He held her so close he worried he might be hurting her, but she never winced or pulled back. Then everyone was crying, even Ruth.

It defied belief or explanation. She loved him before they ever met, and he was overwhelmingly lost in love for her within a week of their meeting!

Traditional wedding ceremonies declare, "What God has brought together, let no man put asunder." God alone had brought them from such different circles that they never would have met otherwise, tying them together with a cord of love. It made no sense, but it made them perfect for each other, complete together!

CHAPTER 10

A few minutes later, after the tears were done, the elder woman excused herself, citing a need to go to her room and lie down. Erin stood, too, thanking her for keeping her company while Allen was resting. Ruth hugged her, saying she enjoyed their visit and looked forward to more.

As she was leaving the room with her back to them, he started to rise. Erin stiff-armed him, knocking him off-balance back onto the couch. Surprised, he looked up with a question forming on his lips, but she had her finger to hers, so he stopped short. She looked back toward the hall where Ruth had disappeared. A moment later they heard the sound of her bedroom door latch as she closed it.

Her eyes were bright as she turned and stated, "We need to talk," then settled down next to him.

"About what?"

"About this," she said, reaching around him. With one hand on the back of his neck and the other pressed to the side of his face, she moved his lips to hers and time stood still. Her kisses were hungry, each one building in intensity from the one before. He wrapped his arms around her, abandoning any attempt at thought, responding blindly as she assaulted his senses!

It must not have lasted long, but he had no point of reference, no awareness of anything other than her body pressed against his and her overwhelming affection. She released him to sit back at some point with a gasp. He felt like he might melt into a puddle as he collapsed back against the couch, attempting to collect his thoughts. They didn't organize easily. He was flushed, his body pulsing with desire as he stared at her in wonder!

She grinned at him. "I have a confession to make," she said. "That's the real reason I didn't take you up on your offer of the guest room. To have you so close in the next room all night long – I didn't trust myself.

"You asked me if it was wrong for a strong partner to take advantage of one who is not as strong, to give into the temptation. I said yes, it is, and I stand by my answer; but now you know how much I want you! If I wake up aroused, sleepy and not thinking clearly, things might happen before I could regain my self-control! I don't want to muck up what we have or cause you any shame!"

"I wouldn't let that happen," he tried to reassure her.

She was not deterred. "You think so, but you couldn't stop me just now, could you?"

He realized he couldn't even think straight a minute ago. She was right; if she hadn't stopped, he would have had no chance! The thought boggled him, she could have taken him on his own couch before he could even think to try to stop it!

She saw the expression on his face as the realization hit home and nodded.

"I didn't lie when I said I would make use of the motel pool and weight room, but those things aren't necessities. I'm not so stuck-up as to refuse an invitation simply because those facilities are not available. You just confessed your love for me; my emotions are boiling over right now. I had to show you how I feel! I choose you because I want you, remember? Now you know how intense my desire is!"

"I – whoa! I've never been one to discount a woman's ability simply due to her gender, but I never considered! Is it possible? Can a woman really rape a man?"

She smiled wolfishly, answering his question with another, "You were married a long time. Young couples experiment. Sooner or later they play with that thought. What was your experience?"

Now that took him back a lot of years, but again she was right. The subject had come up.

"I learned that once sex was underway, if she chose to take control, I couldn't regain it, at least when she was serious about staying in control. It happened more than once, enough to establish it wasn't a fluke." He paused, "Is that really rape? We were playing; I wasn't fighting to escape like my life depended on it. I certainly didn't want to hurt her."

"No, that wasn't rape, just playful sex. When I first started wrestling, I worked for a company as a novice learning the ropes. There were two women working there who were real veterans in the business. Their locker room talk sounded just like conceited guys talking about their conquests in their off time, describing how they lured in men they took a shine to, got them alone and forced them against their will. I was young and it sounded stupid to me, so I thought it was just trash talk.

"One day, ownership took the whole company to dinner at a nice restaurant to celebrate a boost in sales. While we were there, this big nicely dressed man came in with a woman I assumed was his wife. The hostess was about to seat them at a table near ours when he saw us. He turned white as a sheet, literally shook where he stood!

"I heard laughter nearby. It was those two women, looking at him, then each other. He almost ran out of the restaurant, ignoring his wife and the hostess. My coworkers nearly laughed themselves out of their chairs! Right then I knew that what I had heard them say was true. They were rapists, sexual predators and proud of it!

"The thought was repulsive, yet kind of fascinating at the same time, but that man's shame was not funny to anyone but them. I couldn't stand being around them after that, so I soon moved on to another employer."

"Nasty, two women ganging up on one man!" he said.

"No," Erin corrected him, "their locker room talk wasn't recounting shared experiences. They were informing each other of their individual exploits, trying to top each other's feats. One of them victimized that man; I never knew which one." She let that sink in.

"Why didn't he report the crime?" he wondered.

"Think about it. Rape is very personal; most women are too afraid or ashamed to report it. It's usually his word against hers, so it boils down to whatever evidence is recovered to successfully prosecute the crime. Her cooperation requires she revisit that trauma at least twice, once for police and once for the court, when she desperately wants to forget it. It's like reliving a nightmare over and over!

"But it's crazier for a man. A female victim can remember the violence of the act to help her keep in mind she was assaulted. A female rapist needs to employ a measure of seduction to bring about a physical response from her victim, without which she can't succeed. I'm not talking about sodomy; that's something else.

"If she gets that response, it creates the illusion that he is consenting to the act. The human body is built to respond to the opposite sex, so inducing a response isn't that difficult, even when the subject is unwilling. It's like you are betrayed by your own body! His seduction makes him much less certain afterwards whether he really was raped.

"He is ashamed to come forward, just like a female victim; but he also faces a crushing and well-founded fear of ridicule. Society doesn't acknowledge this kind of crime exists, so a serious investigation is unlikely. The crime is even less likely to be prosecuted, but the accusation will make him a laughingstock!

"If this 'impossible' crime is prosecuted, there's no guarantee of a conviction. He will almost inevitably conclude that he needs to suck it up and write it off as sex gone bad. It's ugly because there's no closure! He is traumatized, convinced no one will understand; while the woman who did it is free to rape again, with pretty much zero risk of ever being held accountable."

"You sound sympathetic. Given what you do, that seems a bit contradictory," he observed.

"Why? I don't hate guys. How can I? Horny egotistical men are the market to which session wrestlers cater. Without them, we'd have to find another line of work! Few women are interested in watching us wrestle.

"Allen, no one should be deprived of legal recourse when they are victimized! That leads to people resorting to illegal means of seeking justice. Ask any hunter; the most dangerous animal is one that is wounded and cornered!"

"I continue to be astounded by your sensibility, Erin." She grinned. "I thought women are supposed to be overly emotional, rather than so pragmatic and logical. You are messing with the stereotype, you know!"

Now she laughed outright, "I'm okay with that. Kissing you breathless was emotional, nothing but an act of passion; so yeah, we're pretty emotional! However, we can scheme and connive circles around guys, because we are dangerously clever! Some of us are downright evil.

Those are the kind that pose a threat to others and should be locked up for their crimes.

"Now I have a question," she added. "Does the Bible address rape?"

"Not in so many words. The word isn't mentioned, but three of the Ten Commandments lay out precepts that leave no doubt that it is wrong. 'Love your neighbor as yourself,' precludes committing violent acts against him or her. 'You shall not covet anything that is your neighbor's,'; the first thing mentioned is his wife. If a girl isn't married, she is still your neighbor's daughter, not to be taken without consent. 'You shall not commit adultery,'; that's self-explanatory."

"What penalties does it impose?" she wanted to know.

"The Law of God had different penalties, depending on the crime. If the girl was unmarried, the act constituted marriage with some stiff reparations, not to mention a distrustful father-in-law who would probably kill you if his daughter indicated she was being abused afterward. It was the original shotgun wedding! For taking another man's wife, the penalty was stoning. If she was cheating on her husband, both offenders were stoned."

"Ouch! That seems like overkill," she exclaimed.

"God was making clear that He is holy; He cannot abide sin. For Him to remain in their midst, sin had to be put away without compromise. Of course, an imperfect people could not keep a perfect Law, so God eventually had to distance Himself or destroy them. He distanced Himself until Jesus came to die on the cross. The perfect sacrifice for sin provided closure for the Law, so sin can be forgiven if one receives Christ."

She looked thoughtful, so he went a bit further. "There is an instance of rape in scripture that comes to mind. Amnon raped his half-sister Tamar, then drove her away; both were children of King David. He should have held him accountable, but he chose to ignore the crime.

"Tamar's brother Absalom murdered Amnon for revenge. Having lost respect for his father, who didn't hold him accountable, either, he decided to overthrow him. That led to a civil war in which Absalom was killed. The consequences of David overlooking sin cost him two sons while Israel mourned their fallen in a war that never should have happened.

"As for a woman raping a man, the closest thing in scripture is in Genesis. Joseph was a slave in Potiphar's house when the man's wife came on to him. She grabbed his garment and he shucked it off, fleeing from her naked. She told her husband Joseph tried to rape her.

"A slave had no rights. Potiphar could have killed him; as captain of Pharaoh's guard, there is no way he was squeamish! I suspect he knew the kind of woman he had married, because he instead threw Joseph into prison. I don't think he put him behind bars so much to lock him up, as to keep his wife from getting to him!"

"He was lucky," Erin noted. "If she had grabbed something other than his garment, I doubt he would have escaped from her. I like these stories; you make them interesting."

Allen chuckled, "You're biased. You just like talking with me."

She had a small smile on her face.

He added, "There is nothing I would rather do than spend my time with you, so it's mutual."

She leaned forward to put her arms around his neck again. "My Sweet Talker," she murmured as she kissed him.

CHAPTER 11

They went to Bass Pro to walk around for awhile. When she went shopping the week before, she didn't take time to look around, but she saw enough to make her curious. Now that she wasn't alone, she wanted a closer look. They walked the complex together, taking in the sights, enjoying each other's company.

Plans were made to go back the following day to see the aquarium and wildlife museum. Before they left, she made a single purchase, a small bag of locally made candy, after he agreed to try it with her. It was good, but very sweet; a little went a long way.

They returned home to check on Ruth, who was still resting in her room. She wasn't a shut-in, but she didn't go out much because outings left her exhausted. They decided to go to a Japanese steakhouse. He left a note, promising to bring her back a plate.

Erin seemed delighted at the experience; Allen got a kick out of watching her. When she broke out her bank card, he didn't say anything this time, but he felt awkward. She looked at him with that piercing gaze, then leaned against him, putting one arm around his shoulders and the other hand on his knee. "Thank you for letting me do this," she said.

"Thank you," he replied, "this was a real treat."

"My pleasure; I had a blast!"

They got Ruth's food before heading home. She was up this time and pleased with what was brought for her. They left her eating to go to the living room, where they decided to put on a movie. Having kicked off their shoes (well, his shoes, her boots) they started to cuddle up on the couch when he had a thought. He asked her to stand a moment while he grabbed a couple of throw pillows and positioned them at one end.

She wondered aloud, "What are you doing?"

"Making my dream come true, or at least part of it," as he laid down, beckoning her to join him. His back was against the couch back with her back to him as she settled in, then he put his right arm around her midsection and pulled her close. His left arm was under her neck, her soft blonde hair like silk light upon it. She pressed back into him, covering his arm around her waist with both of hers. It wasn't sexual, but it was perfect, holding her that way.

She didn't say anything for a minute, so he picked up the remote to start the movie. A slight shake of her shoulders surprised him.

He stopped short to ask, "Are you okay?" raising his head to see her face.

She turned to look up at him. There were tears in her eyes!

"I really am home, aren't I?"

He leaned down to kiss her softly, "You are, as far as I'm concerned."

With a happy smile, she turned back and inched down a bit, then nuzzled the back of her head into his neck. He laid his head above hers, then heard her say, "Please don't ever let me go."

"You've got a deal," he whispered.

After the movie, they kissed goodnight. She left for the motel, after confirming plans to see the aquarium the next day. His bed felt empty after holding her on the couch. He reminded himself that he would see her tomorrow.

As he said his nightly prayer, he thanked the Lord for His kindness in bringing her to him and for the bond of love they shared that could only have come from Him. Peace surrounded him as he dropped off to sleep.

They spent the next day at the aquarium and wildlife museum, taking in the sights while basking in each other's presence. She seemed like a kid in a candy store; her enthusiasm kept him smiling most of the time. She noticed his amusement and wanted to know why he looked at her that way. He guessed she was self-conscious. He expressed how he loved watching her excitement.

"I don't get out much," she admitted. "The business absorbed my attention; besides, doing things alone didn't appeal to me. Where's the fun in that?"

"Didn't you date?" Allen wondered.

"Not for some years. It's disappointing when you fail to connect at the heart level over and over. Then *you* started showing up in my dreams. My imagination was captured; reality couldn't compete with the happiness I dreamed up!

"Finding you rocked my world; it still does. I don't think you are ever going to stop rocking my world, Allen! I love it; I hope it never stops!"

"So, you're a workaholic, then. I wondered how a California girl could miss out getting a tan," he teased.

"Humph! Look who's talking, white boy," she replied with mock indignation.

"That's me, but I don't have those famous beaches to hang out on. If you don't go there, they must be overrated, I suppose."

"No, they're not! I've just been too busy to make use of them. If you keep giving me a hard time, I might just have to show you what I've been too busy doing to get there! And I don't think you are ready for that, mister!"

"Peace!" he said quickly, "I don't care to risk life and limb over this discussion."

She laughed.

"Besides, I find your color very attractive. I'd prefer you didn't change it."

"That's better. We'll be palefaces together, a matched set," she chuckled.

"But you use makeup!" He raised his right hand, "How! Me Foot In Mouth, you Warpaint!" That cracked her up. It was a fun outing.

They stopped at the house about 5:30 p.m. to find Ruth making dinner, so they hung out to eat with her, pork chops, broccoli, mashed potatoes and gravy. It was a great time visiting while they ate. Erin volunteered them to clean up. He put the leftovers away as Erin washed the dishes, reassuring Ruth they had this and thanking her for the home cooked meal.

When they finished, they joined her in the living room to talk some more, until Ruth announced she was going back to her room to rest. She said goodnight and hugged Erin when she stood up with her, asking her if she was having fun.

"So much! I'm thinking about coming back and moving in with you!" She giggled.

"Well, come on," his mom replied without missing a beat, "we have a guest room with your name on it. I can always use another dishwasher!" They both laughed, then Ruth retired for the night.

CHAPTER 12

E rin and Allen discussed what to do next. She suggested going for a swim at her motel, so that's where they went. He changed in her bathroom. She reminded him of his teasing earlier.

"You have some nerve, calling me pale! What are you, some kind of vampire?" She grinned, then winked as he blushed.

"Yeah, well, I don't wear shorts or take off my shirt outside, so I don't get much sun," he grumbled, embarrassed.

She kissed him on the cheek on her way to the bathroom to change. "I understand, but you just forfeited any right to tease me further, white boy!" She chuckled as the door shut.

Allen wasn't particularly attentive to how others dress, unless something about it stood out to him. Other than the day he met her, she dressed stylishly, but low-key. She seemed partial to pants that fit nicely, not tight or baggy, with short sleeve sweaters that indicated her figure without emphasizing it. Then there were those ever-present dressy boots she favored.

When she came out of the bathroom, she had a terry cloth cover-up over her swimwear, but her legs were exposed. He was captivated! The ski pants she wore the day they met had hinted at perfect proportions, but they seemed chiseled from marble, only they flexed with definition at every step. He couldn't take his eyes off of them!

Thankfully, she seemed oblivious as he stared, the flip-flops on her feet making little smacking sounds as she walked to her nightstand to retrieve her room key. She took his hand as she passed on her way to the door, saying, "I'm looking forward to hearing what you think of my suit when we get to the pool."

He just hoped his heart didn't fail at the sight of what was *in* the suit!

When they arrived, they approached a table. As soon as she released his hand to untie her cover-up, he pulled the towel off his shoulders, laid it on the table, turned and jumped into the pool as she hollered, "Hey!"

The sound cut off as he went under; the water was colder than anticipated. He came up shivering. He grabbed the side, smoothed his hair back, then looked up to see her standing above him in a bikini, looking irritated.

"You were supposed to tell me what you think of my outfit first!"

"Sorry," he replied, turning red as his body had the predictable reaction to the sight. Being Monday night, no one else was at the pool. He was glad for that!

He shivered as he took in the view.

Her figure was as perfect as he thought it would be, but there was a wiriness that hinted at well-developed muscle just below the skin. Despite his teasing earlier, she actually had a light tan that seemed to accentuate that musculature. There was no part of her that wasn't well developed. The bikini was blue. A stray thought marked that it matched her eyes; as expected, *it* barely gained his notice.

He wiggled his fingers in a 'come here' motion and raised up as she knelt down, obviously peeved. He confessed in a low tone, "Erin, I jumped in so I wouldn't embarrass myself! Please don't be angry."

Noticing he was beet red, her face softened. She glanced down, then back up, "Oh!" A huge smile lit her face, "Then you *do* like my suit!"

"I love it. You could wear a giant banana peel and I would like it. Will you please get in here with me?"

She laughed, "Coming, Sweet Talker."

She walked around to the low dive board, then dove in headfirst. Homing in like a torpedo, she came up directly before him, poking a finger into his navel as she did. That startled him into releasing the lip of the pool. As he began to sink, she moved in close. Erin reached around to grip the edge with a hand on either side of him, while her legs wrapped around to pin his body to the pool wall. With nothing else to hold onto, he reached around to hook his hands over her shoulders from behind.

"Oh, what to do with you now?" she mused, laughing, kissing him twice. "You really do like my outfit, don't you?" There was no way she could miss his response to her now!

Shivering, self-conscious, he was trapped in her grip, utterly vulnerable and they both knew it!

He asked, "You are still wearing one, aren't you?"

That got a hearty laugh, "Of course I am, silly. I told you I'm not going muck things up by taking advantage of you. Though I admit it's tempting. It would be *so easy*," she teased, "but it still wouldn't be right."

She released him. Taking his hand, she moved to the side, carefully placing it back on the lip of the pool. Holding the edge with her hand next to his, she leaned forward, stopping short of a kiss this time, letting him meet her partway. He was grateful for that. He kissed her twice while they embraced there.

Then she took off, so he had to chase her. The pursuit turned into a workout; it was more than a decade since he had been swimming. He quickly ran out of steam. It became apparent that she was very proficient in the water. After he slowed down, she swam the pool end to end three times, without even breathing hard. Her conditioning earned his immediate respect. He told her so; it got him a grin and another kiss.

She began swimming laps, giving him a peck on the lips every time she returned, making a game of it. He was at the shallow end, enjoying her game, when she disappeared partway back. He was still looking for her when she rose up beneath him, propelling his two hundred forty-pound frame into the air to splash down several feet away!

He whirled around to find her laughing so hard she was holding her sides and struggling to stand. He was in shock that she could do that, but couldn't help laughing at something she found so funny.

He walked over to take her hand. Turning her around, he put his arms around her, as he had on the couch the night before. She relaxed back into his embrace with a happy little "Hmmm," having no idea what he intended. He raised his knee under her backside, lifting her little frame up off the pool floor; then, with his hands on her shoulders, shoved her down and forward in his own patented dunk!

She let out a squawk that cut off sharply as she went under, moving forward at high speed, butt first. He was proud of that dunk he developed so many years ago! It leaves one having to stop forward momentum, then turn over to regain footing, which gives him time to enjoy the moment as his victim flails around trying to recover. There is nothing graceful about that recovery!

She got her legs under her several feet away. Pushing her hair back, she looked at him with a fierce smile. "So, it's like that, huh?"

"Yep," he replied with a chuckle.

She took three steps forward, launching upward and past him to grab his head as she went by. The rest of him followed, being attached, so he went down. She released him and was gone as he worked to right himself. He stood, wiping his eyes to find her only a foot in front of him.

As soon as he saw her, she poked his belly button again. He jerked back involuntarily, bending forward a bit. She tucked his head under her shoulder and fell backward, pulling him under while kicking his feet out from under him; then once more, she was gone. Again, he was struggling to get his feet under him, with no idea where she went.

With an effort, he stood, casting about for her with no luck. As he started to turn, he felt her knee lift him, then her hands on his shoulders shoving him down and forward, butt first. She used his own dunk against him! As he slid through the water ingloriously trying to right himself, he realized she had his number. He was done. It was tough regaining his balance; it must have showed on his face. She was standing in front of him in easy reach as he cleared his eyes.

"Had enough?" she asked, smiling.

"Yeah, I'm waterlogged," he coughed. She held him close while he coughed it out, then they climbed out of the pool.

"Where did you learn that last dunk you used on me?" he asked.

"From you, when you used it on me," she came back. "Where else?" Seeing his puzzlement, she expounded, "I'm a very quick study when I observe a maneuver I like.

Besides, I was determined to give you a taste of your own medicine!"

With a wry smile, he told her, "Well, I guess that makes me feel better. I thought I invented that move, but when you did it to me, it seemed I was mistaken."

They were toweled off now and starting back toward the room.

She chuckled, "As far as I know, you did invent it. I haven't seen it before today. I hereby christen it the Allen dunk," she laughed. "It will be put to good use the next time we have a dunking contest!"

"Nuh-uh! I'm not gonna get into one of those again with you! Once was enough!"

She opened the door and entered her room, grinning, "C'mon now, you're not afraid of *me*, a girl half your size, are you?"

"When she swims like Jaws and can toss me across the pool – let's just say I'm cautious, okay?"

She broke into fresh laughter. "The look on your face was priceless! I wish I could have snapped a picture."

"I'm glad you didn't. It was embarrassing enough being there!"

They took turns in the shower, getting dressed in the bathroom, then discussed what to do. They opted to go out for a soda and perhaps a snack, ending up at the convenience store where they met. With that happy memory, they held hands as they shopped and kept glancing at each other, smiling.

CHAPTER 13

Returning to the car, they exchanged another look and Erin commenced laughing. Amused, Allen asked what was so funny. She said they were, acting like a couple of love-struck teenagers in the store, or didn't he notice? He agreed, stipulating he saw no problem with that; besides, it was her fault! She stiffened as he went on to say no one else brought out this kind of behavior in him, so she *must* be to blame!

She started to say something when he leaned over to kiss her, cutting her off. As soon as their lips parted, she tried to talk again, but he cut her off again the same way. He felt her giggle as their arms wrapped around each other. The kisses melded together into one long exchange.

He stopped a moment to inquire, "Were you saying something?"

Only an inch apart, she shook her head. "Huh-uh."

He went back to kissing her; there was no mistaking her response. The warmth they shared on the couch this morning was coming back, only this time he was leading.

She seemed to be melting into his arms. He was losing himself to her embrace when she stopped, barely breaking contact. Her arms were around his neck as her eyes bored into his.

"You *do* know where this is going, don't you?" she asked softly.

It sank in slowly as her gaze held him motionless. "Oh," he responded, "*Oh!*"

He would have jerked backward, but her arms didn't give an inch.

"I'm so sorry!"

"Don't be sorry. I'm not complaining. I just want to be sure you are conscious of your decision before going further. Is this what you want?" Her eyes never looked away.

He was mortified. "Erin, I am so sorry! Premarital sex is a huge no-no for me. Sin would drive a wedge between the Lord and me. I can't do that! I was having fun and got carried away. You are irresistible to me, but I didn't plan to lead you on."

"I got it," she said, putting a finger on his lips to stop him. "That's what I thought, knowing something of your beliefs. No harm done; I'm not to the point of no return yet, but it wouldn't have taken much more. It comforts me to know your attraction to me is as strong as mine to you!"

"If you only knew-"

She cut him off with a little peck on the lips. "I do; believe me, I do. I don't want to stop, Allen. It was respect for you alone that compelled me to interrupt what was happening! You seem a bit naïve, but I'm not going to let that lead you into anything you'll regret with me. I value you too much to let that happen!"

Tears welled up in his eyes. "I love you so much, Erin!"

Her hand went to his cheek, "I love you, too." She gave an involuntary shiver and sat back in the seat, muttering

"Gotta cool down." She took a deep breath. He sat back, following suit.

After a moment and a sip of her drink, he heard her say blandly, "So, when do you want to get married?"

His jaw dropped; his surprise was obvious. The look on his face caused her to roar with laughter!

After a moment, he caught her contagious amusement, shaking his head. "Man, you are *bold*! I had no idea you were joking," he replied, still laughing with her.

"Shy girls don't get into my line of work," she stated, slowly recovering, "and who said I was joking? It was your expression that cracked me up. I'm completely serious!"

He was too at that point, speechless and incredulous. His face was an open book.

She went on, "You don't agree with premarital sex; okay, I can accommodate that. I'm willing to honor your convictions as the weaker vessel in this relationship. However, I don't think there's anything wrong with wanting to know *how long* you expect me to wait before jumping your bones, boy!"

What on Earth could he say to that? He was at a total loss.

She leaned forward to cup his face with her hand. "You look like you're drowning, so let me throw you a lifeline. I don't have to have an answer now. You are worth waiting for!" she said softly. "Just don't keep me waiting too long, okay?"

Feeling shaky, he took a deep breath, "Okay."

That didn't rock his world, it rocked *him*! It put him completely off-balance. His thoughts were a jumble as he tried to work through what she said. She asked if he was alright. He said yes, it's just that she gave him a lot to think about. She asked what he wanted to do.

He thought about it, "Honestly, I need some quiet time to process what you said. Would you mind taking me home?"

She did so with an instant, "Sure," that bespoke hurt. The short ride home was made in silence until they pulled into the driveway. Erin put the car in park, then turned to him. "I know I can come on strong sometimes. I didn't say anything I didn't mean, but please tell me I haven't ruined what we have!"

He turned toward her, took her hand. "You haven't ruined anything, Erin. I don't think you could, unintentionally. Everything between us has happened so fast that I haven't... considered marriage yet. Mom said your dreams gave you a head start in determining your feelings for me."

She nodded slowly, then more emphatically as she absorbed what was said.

"We haven't been together 10 days, so please bear with me. I hate that I have to ask for space when you've come more than a thousand miles to see me; but you don't understand the effect you have on me. I don't think straight when I'm with you! You fill my senses into overload more than any drug could! I am yours, but it must be my willing gift, not the state I find myself in because I'm blown away by you. Am I making any sense?" He so needed her to understand.

"Yeah, I think so. I just don't want to lose you," she said.

"There's no risk of that, Erin. You have me hook, line and sinker; just give me time to catch up to where you are in this relationship."

"How much time do you need? Should I go home and come back when you call?" she asked.

"Dear God, no! If I need that much time, I'm definitely not ready to commit to you. I'm just talking overnight, okay?"

She smiled, visibly relaxing, "Are you sure that's enough?"

"Not totally, but if I need an extension, I'm talking to the right person, aren't I?"

She nodded and smiled again.

"I love it when you smile at me that way," he said. "I know I don't want to go through life deprived of that!"

Her eyes brightened; the smile widened.

"My experience is that it's wise to sleep on major decisions, let the morning bring new perspective. Do you eat eggs and sausage?"

A little confused, she replied, "Yeah."

"How about I make breakfast for us about 10 in the morning? I make a Southwest Scramble that's pretty good, if I say so myself, with chopped tomatoes, onions and green chile."

"I'll be here with an appetite. Should I bring anything?"

"Just your beautiful self, with that smiling face that lights up my life!"

"My Sweet Talker!" she breathed, giving him a quick kiss. Before pulling away, she asked in a tone just above a whisper, "We're gonna be okay, aren't we?"

"You bet we are! If I don't let go and you don't let go, with God's blessing we are a lock!" After a long lingering kiss, they said goodnight.

CHAPTER 14

Whether it was his screwed-up sleep schedule or all the thoughts filling his over-active brain (probably both were factors), he only had 4 hours of sleep that night. He prayed and pondered what amounted to her proposal, wondering if she really grasped the weight of what she had put out there when the words seemed so spontaneous.

The thought that possibly he wasn't ready to commit was laid to rest in short order. Marriage would not be a chore, not with Erin, considering how strong his feelings were for her. He had some questions to discuss with her concerning their future, but only one that required an answer she couldn't help provide.

For that one, he received help when Ruth went to the kitchen to make her breakfast, about 6 a.m. When he heard her stirring around, he went in to greet her.

"Good morning! You're up early," she observed. "How was your time with Erin last night?"

"Wonderful as always, Ma," he said. "She asked me to marry her!"

Her jaw dropped, "She proposed to you?"

He nodded.

Ruth shook her head, "Times sure have changed."

"They have," he agreed, "but you did say that she would be the initiator in our relationship."

"I guess I did, at that. Tell me how it went and what you answered."

He recounted how they kissed until Erin stopped him with her question that put him on the spot, followed by the conversation that led up to *the* question. Ruth laughed so hard he thought she might fall off the desk chair she used in that room. He turned a bit red; it didn't seem funny to him.

"One thing about it, son; you will never have to wonder what is on her mind! Ready or not, she will tell you right up front!"

He grinned sheepishly, "You have a point."

"I have to hand it to you, you didn't run away. Any man who didn't love her dearly would have, at that point."

"I think she thought she had scared me off, when I asked her to take me home." He related the remainder of their exchange, including what passed between them in the driveway.

"You two make a fun story, that's for sure," she noted. "The breakfast invitation was inspired, letting her know you didn't expect her to wait for a call she was afraid might never come or meet at a restaurant where you might not show up."

He started to object, but she held up her hand, "I know you wouldn't do that to her, but her imagination would not have given her any peace." He hadn't thought of that.

"Have you used the time you requested to come to any conclusions?"

"Mom, I want to spend my life with her. It has been black and white since I was served with divorce papers; it seems pointless, drab. Erin has brought the color back into my existence, given me reason to look forward to tomorrow. I haven't had that in a very long time; even when I wasn't alone, I felt like I was for quite a few years. This woman wants to be with me. It makes life worth living!

"But she hasn't received Christ. Scripture warns us not to be unequally yoked with an unbeliever. I'll give her up if the Lord wants me too, but it won't be much of a life without her, you know?" His face was hot, his heart breaking as the words came out.

"Oh, honey! Don't do that to yourself! Hey," she rolled over to him, took his hand, "the Lord brought you two together, revealing Himself to her in the process. He is working on her, has been before you ever met. He knows she won't refuse Him, or He never would have orchestrated your coming together. Follow your heart, having faith that He will finish what He started! 'He who began a good work will be faithful to complete it,' remember?"

He managed a weak smile as he felt a weight lift off him.

"The Lord's warning is for believers dabbling with sexual sin. Sin breaks fellowship with God, giving the devil opportunity to deceive them into thinking they can legitimize what they have done by making it legal. 'Unless the Lord builds the house, they labor in vain who build it.' Can you imagine moving into a house that you *know* will someday collapse on you? The Lord issued the warning to steer us from that trap."

He hugged her tight. "Thanks, Mom. That's the perspective I needed." For the first time since last night with Erin, he felt like he could breathe.

"Now I want to know the answer to Erin's question: when do you want to marry her? If I need to find a new place to live, how much time do I have to make arrangements?"

He was shocked! "What, you won't take your own advice? I'm not gonna put you out! And Erin won't, either. She told you if you needed anything, just ask, remember? You need to have some faith, too, okay?"

"Okay," she said weakly, tears running down her cheeks. "Let me know what you two decide after you talk."

"We will, Ma. Don't worry; God is doing a good thing here, not just for me and Erin, but for you, too. If I must have faith, you have to stand with me on this! Erin hasn't come to faith yet. You and I need each other!"

"We do, don't we?" she smiled bravely. "Okay, let's see where the Lord leads from here."

Allen did get a short nap before getting up to prepare for Erin's arrival. He was excited and at peace simultaneously, having an answer for her, while feeling like he had both feet solidly grounded. She arrived ten minutes early. When he opened the door, all the wind went out of him.

For the first time since they met, she was wearing a little black dress that showed her shoulders and snugly fit her figure. It was not overpowering, going almost to the knee, where black hose continued down to black high heels; but it was very feminine, much more formal than he expected. Her lioness mane of blonde hair was brushed out to frame her face, which seemed to glow in his sight. He was dumbstruck!

After a moment, she said, "May I come in?"

"Y-yeah," he replied, stepping back.

She stepped in abreast of him in the hallway. "What do you think?" She raised her arms, turning a bit both ways to model her outfit.

"This is for me?"

She had no idea the question was more aimed for the Lord than for her, so she answered, "Of course, silly. Who else?"

"Wow! I... wow!"

"Then you like?"

"Erin, you take my breath away! Barbara Eden had nothing on you! Oh, wow!"

She blushed, "I don't know about that. I think you're kind of biased, too. But I'll take it! Thank you."

He hugged her close, "You are so beautiful!"

As he pulled back, she chided him, "What, no kiss?"

"I didn't want to mess up your makeup -"

She cut him off with a hard kiss of her own. "*You* don't ever need to worry about that," he was told.

"Okay," he acknowledged. Taking her hand, he led her to the kitchen while asking, "Why did you get so dolled up for breakfast at home? I'm definitely not complaining, just so you know."

She laughed, "Actually, you gave me the idea. When I asked if you wanted me to bring anything, you said I should bring my beautiful self. I decided to take it literally, thought it would be fun to see if I could knock your socks off. Did it work?"

"Boy, did it ever! I thought I had managed to get my feet back firmly on the ground, but the sight of you has put fresh butterflies in my stomach!"

She giggled mischievously.

"I'm going to try to cook anyway," he added.

"I hope so; I'm hungry!" she declared.

Having the ingredients laid out, he assured her it would be ready in a few minutes. As he turned to the range, he continued, "By the way, concerning your question last night – how about August, four months from now?"

He never heard her get up, but suddenly he was yanked around by one arm and she was there, kissing him hard, crushing his body against hers. Time was starting to stand still for him again when she broke the lip lock.

Her face beamed, "You just made me the happiest woman in the world! You wait and see, I'm gonna make you the happiest man in the world too, over and over again!"

His eyes watered, "Erin, you already have; that's the truth. But if you don't let go, I'm gonna burn breakfast!"

She released him, stepping back with a giggle, "Don't do that!" She was at his elbow until he finished cooking, hovering so close he had to be careful not to bump into her. Had he not been preparing their meal, he didn't think she would have turned loose of him in the first place!

When he handed her a plate, she took it and sat back down. He joined her, asked the blessing, then they dug in.

She made a big deal of his simple meal, which he certainly appreciated. When she asked if he had more cooking skills, he laughed, telling her she should have inquired about that before proposing!

"True," she chuckled, "but it's not like I've done it before. That's not something a girl can practice, 'cause once the guy says yes, practice is over!"

Conceding the point, he revealed that he had a limited repertoire of maybe half a dozen dishes. She said she enjoyed cooking but didn't often take time to do it.

She then shifted gears, "Why August?"

"When I prayed about it, that's the month that stood out."

"*That's* the only reason?"

"For selecting that month, yes; but setting the date a ways off makes sense. We have a lot of decisions to discuss. If we flew to Vegas to marry today, it might be fun; but there's no bed bigger than a twin in this house for us to share! Besides, I'm scheduled to work tonight. I don't want to be gone on our wedding night!"

"No, that's unacceptable to me, too! Besides, what if Miss Ruth needs help while we're gone? Okay, I see your point," she admitted. "I guess it's time to come back down to earth."

"A certain very intelligent friend of mine recently assured me that we would make it through difficult circumstances by leaning on each other, because neither of us is alone anymore," he reminded her.

The sparkle came back into her eyes as she slowly smiled, "She sounds like one smart cookie."

"I certainly think so. She impresses me every time we speak." He inclined toward her. "Hey, I don't like waiting, either; but you are my comfort and my reward. You're so worth waiting for, too! Just think, two weeks ago neither of us knew the other existed; yet, now we are beginning to plan a future we couldn't envision back then!"

He stood and offered his hand. She took it, rising to embrace him; those lovely blue eyes searched his.

"It's crazy, isn't it?"

He kissed her gently, nodding as she rested her head against his chest.

"I couldn't ask for a better outcome. I can be patient if you are my reward, Sweet Talker."

He led her to the couch, where they settled next to each other. "What kind of wedding do you want?" he asked.

She looked up quickly, grinning.

CHAPTER 15

The day went by swiftly as they planned a million details; so many, in fact, that it became a relief to have months ahead to work them all out. He told Erin that while it did not matter to him where they would live, he had two compelling reasons for staying in the area: Ruth had a good doctor she would not want to leave, and the clinic that prescribed his insulin had a program that made it affordable.

Erin readily agreed that Ruth would stay with them. When they brought her up to speed, Erin expressed that she looked forward to having a mom, then was invited to start calling her Mom, which teared her up. She asked if they were going to do rings; Allen said they hadn't had time to even consider that.

Erin loved the idea, so they went shopping. She told him flatly that she had this covered. The topic wasn't open to discussion. She wanted his input, not his money, so keep his wallet in his pocket!

He asked why the hard line? Holding his hand, she told him she understood how this might feel awkward for him, but she was determined that they would have a symbol to remind them of their bond to each other before she had to leave in the morning. "Like the Allen Dunk I paid you back, this *is* going to happen, so just accept it."

Her forcefulness was like being doused with cold water. It made him uncomfortable with her for the first time. He prayed quietly about it. The thought came to mind, *She doesn't know any other way to make her point, so she is taking a firm stand. Thank her for her generosity and don't take offense to her approach; she means well.*

Erin was very open and pleasant as they talked about other things, not even getting annoyed that he couldn't direct her to jewelry stores. He told her he was sorry, but not having any need for them, he had never paid any attention to locations. She brought up a short list on her smart phone, then read a couple of addresses that he recognized, asking if he could direct her. It pleased him when she didn't opt to google directions, rather than rely on him.

They didn't find anything they liked at the first store. The second store was pay dirt, though expensive. He kept the Lord's counsel in mind, making no attempt to help pay, but did express the cost was more than he expected. She produced her bank card, ran it, then turned to kiss him.

"You're worth every penny and more to me, love," she said.

She took the larger ring in one hand, while holding out the other, "May I?"

He put his left hand in hers. She slid it onto his ring finger with a grin, "Now that's better."

He picked up her ring off the counter, held out his left hand with a flourish, "Would you do me the honor, milady?"

She giggled, putting her left hand in his, then he pressed the ring onto her finger.

"Thank you, kind sir," she said as another giggle escaped her lips.

"Seriously, thank you, Erin. I don't know what else to say."

They were walking out to the car when the lady in the little black dress turned to him. She stepped into his arms, taking him in hers with a warm wet lingering kiss. "Nothing else needs to be said, Allen. Let's go home and show Mom our rings, okay?"

He found himself playing with his ring constantly, not being used to it. During his first marriage, they didn't get one for him until several years into it. At the time, he worked for an oil distributor. Worried that chemicals he handled might damage it, he never got used to wearing it.

This time, Erin put it on his finger, so he decided not to remove it. It was like wearing an attachment to her, so he treasured it. Silly, he supposed, but that's how he felt.

Noticing that she seemed just as fixated with hers made him feel a little less silly. When they would observe the other fiddling with the ring, they grinned at each other, sometimes cracking up laughing.

The day flew by. Painfully aware he had to work that night and that she planned to leave in the morning, all he wanted to do was hold her. He didn't care what else they did, as long as he didn't have to let her go. She never objected or complained, so perhaps she felt it, too. They cuddled together on the couch until she expressed she wanted to go to her motel to change clothes.

Afterward, she said she wanted to show him the weight room. To him, that was pointless (they all look alike); but if it meant being with her, it was fine with him.

It was an eye-opening experience. It was small, as he expected. No one was there in the early afternoon, which didn't surprise him. Her demeanor did; she wanted to know what he could lift! He had no idea, not having used machines in ages, but it wasn't an idle question. She challenged him on the spot to see who could lift more weight!

He asked if she was serious. She was, taking his hand, then leading him to the bench. She postulated that if he could beat her at any lift, the bench press was his best chance! Not being a competitive person, he asked if she was trying to humiliate him. Erin pointed out that they were alone, so no one would know the outcome but them. It would be fun!

Her repeated references to him being the weaker vessel returned to mind. He decided maybe it would be good to show her he was no wimp, so he agreed.

Did they need to warm up? She said since they weren't doing reps, it would be okay if they eased up to their max lifts. He wondered if this woman would be the death of him as he lay down on the bench. The thought crossed his mind that this might not be the last time he would wonder about that!

She asked where to set the weight. He told her it had been so many years since he had done this, he didn't know; how about 120 lbs. to start? He hefted it with no problem, then had her add 20 lbs. He felt that as she watched carefully; it was an exertion. He asked for 20 lbs. more.

She countered, "How about ten first?"

He agreed. It was a good call. It was all he could do to raise it; his arms trembled. He let it down with a clank to sit up, looking at her.

She smiled encouragement, "Not bad, for fifty-six years old and completely out of practice. How long since you lifted?"

"I was in the Navy, so – thirty years ago, a little more, I suppose. I was dinking around, never did it seriously.

You're gonna show me up, aren't you?" he said, rubbing his arms gingerly.

She grinned as she lay down on the bench. She took a couple of breaths and he started to ask what she wanted it set at, when she lifted the 150 lbs. he had struggled with! It wasn't easy for her, but she didn't tremble like he had. She lowered it, then raised it twice more before setting it down. He was pretty sure he couldn't have done that.

He grimaced, "Well, I'm impressed and proud of you, while being aroused and emasculated all at the same time." With a rueful half-smile and a shake of his head, he added, "If you are stronger than I am in the arms, there's no point in crushing my ego further with other lifts. I guess I *am* weaker." It was not easy to admit.

She noticed. Putting her arms around him, she touched his nose playfully. "My being stronger than you doesn't mean you're weak, sweetheart. You said in the pool that you were impressed with my conditioning; that's the difference. My lifestyle demands that I work hard to stay strong and fit; yours doesn't make those demands.

"In no way does that make you inferior! You work to improve the lives of the less fortunate. You are also there for your mom at a time in her life when she needs help. You are a strong, admirable man in ways that matter to me! If I tease you, it's only for fun. Don't think for one minute that I look down on you, because it's not true." She punctuated her statement with a kiss.

"You know," he said slowly, his arms around her now, holding her loosely, "I always thought that by keeping my strength in check, being careful not to hurt my girl, that tenderness was the sexiest thing I had to offer. Now that you're my girl and I'm outclassed, I find myself in strange territory.

"As the stronger partner, her trust was my biggest turn-on, so that's what you will have from me. You said the thought of hurting me made you nauseous. That's *good*; you hold onto that!" he chuckled as she laughed.

"I don't like pain. Pain hurts, whether it's from being run over by a truck or being twisted like a pretzel by a gorgeous woman. I'm trusting you won't hurt me and hope to God you don't get off on another's pain, cause that is a dealbreaker for me!"

"Why, Allen," she grinned with amusement, "I do believe I've intimidated you."

"You have," he admitted, somewhat nervous, "and even if it costs me big, I will not live like that, not now, not ever!"

"Shh! I will never get off on hurting you, Sweet Talker; it would be like shooting myself in the foot. You are a part of me! I can't hurt you without feeling your pain; there's no fun in that! It is true that my strength and skills are geared toward making men cave, but you pose a whole new challenge for me.

"Three of your four responses to seeing my strength were good. I like that you were impressed and proud of me! I look forward to exploring the ways in which it arouses you (that sounds like fun!) I will *never* leave you feeling emasculated, because I am a woman. Beating men is my business, but no one can make a man feel glad to be a man more than a woman, and that will always be my pleasure! Am I making sense?"

"Complete sense! I feel silly talking about this. I really do trust you." They started heading for the car.

"I know," she said. "It's not misplaced, I promise you. Don't feel silly for talking to me about anything ever, okay? I always want us to be upfront about our thoughts and feelings, even when they don't make sense. Who else should we share them with, if not each other?"

In the car he asked, "What did you mean, 'I pose a whole new challenge for you'?"

She turned, fixing her gaze on him, then taking his hand in hers. They were still parked, so she could afford to give him her full attention.

"How do I say this? You said you are already broken; I'm beginning to see what you mean. You lack self-confidence," he nodded, "so much so that it pains me to behold. Your vulnerability is winsome and alarming at the same time. I find myself wanting to ride to *your* rescue, to be your knight in shining armor! You are in danger of being crushed, if someone careless gets too close to you. I want to surround you with my love, to shore you up, help you rebuild."

His eyes were watering; both her hands held his.

She chuckled, "I break men for a profession, but with everything in me I want to build you up! How's that for irony? A destroyer becoming a nurturer; that is the challenge I face with you. They say that behind every great man is a strong woman. Buddy, you are marrying a *very* strong woman, so all my strength and my confidence is going to fill in the gaps in yours to make you stronger than you've ever been!"

"Thank you," he whispered, fighting back tears, "I could use that."

"I know, my love. I will never intentionally use my strength or skills to embarrass you before others. When I do assert myself with you, it will always be in private, just between us. Rest assured, you will like the outcome.

"Oh, you might as well know, the bedroom is mine." That wolfish smile was reflected in her eyes. "I will exercise utter control there; that is a fact. I will be disappointed if you don't challenge my control, but you will never take it from me! Nor will you ever regret what happens there, because you are *my* man and you will always leave it knowing you are loved!"

"Darn, now I wish we were getting married tomorrow!" he laughed.

She grinned. "Nope, you're gonna have to wait, Sweet Talker. We're both committed now!

CHAPTER 16

They coordinated with Ruth to bring home barbecue ribs to go with sides she prepared for Erin's last dinner with them. She asked when they would see her next. Erin planned to make it back the next week, but if not, two weeks at the outside.

Ruth said she hoped Erin would consider taking the guest room next time. She smiled wryly at Allen. He smiled back, then she looked down at the ring on her finger before saying she just might, as things stood. As she said earlier, they were both committed to wait for their wedding at this point.

The rings were a constant tangible reminder of their commitment to wait, a kind of safety net against getting caught up in the heat of the moment. He could tell Erin was weighing it in her mind. He wasn't worried; not only did he trust her, he trusted the Lord even more, a reassurance she could not yet understand. Even though he now knew she could overpower him, His care was more than adequate to protect them both!

He wanted her to have the same reassurance that knowing Christ provided him, so he asked if she would like a Bible. Surprised, she said, "That would be great! Do you have one to spare?" He retrieved one, then gave it to her.

She asked if they had any suggestions where to start reading. They agreed the gospels would be best. Allen recommended Matthew but advised glossing over the genealogy at the beginning for the time being.

Ruth told her something that startled her, "Erin, the Bible isn't meant just to be read, like literature. It is meant to be explained by God Himself! Honey, if you ask Him to make it come alive to you before you open it, He will! You don't have to be a Christian for Him to answer this prayer. He always testifies to His truth to anyone willing to hear it, if asked.

"People are judged for their rejection of His word. No one can accept what they never understood in the first place! He knows that, so He provides understanding to anyone who sincerely asks for it."

Erin said plaintively, "I wouldn't know how to approach Him, Mom."

She laughed, "He approached *you*, remember? With more than a thousand dreams of the man who now sits beside you, planning to share his life with you! *Those dreams* were how the Lord approached you. My son is the gift He offered, to get your attention."

Erin's breath caught in her throat; tears began to stream down her cheeks.

Ruth went on, "It is Christ Himself that is courting you, daughter, offering gifts more precious than any man or woman deserves. As much as I love my son, he isn't the best gift the Lord is offering you. He wants to forgive your sins, to come into your heart, so you can be with Him and us for eternity.

"By receiving Allen as your life partner, you made it clear you are willing to hear what God has to say. He is certainly going to help you understand; all you need to do is ask!"

"I don't know what to say!" Erin declared.

Ruth got up to hug her close, "Don't say anything, just think about what I've told you. You're going home a different girl than when you arrived. You now have a man who loves you to share your life with, a future with him that actually gives your retirement appeal, and a new home away from home, so to speak! That's a lot to process! Have you ever accomplished so much in four days' time?"

Tears gave way to laughter, "No, I never have, but you forgot something. I have a Mom now, and I sure am glad! Thanks for putting things in perspective."

Ruth hobbled back to her chair. Wiping her brow, she feigned exhaustion. "A mother's work is never done," she grinned. They all laughed.

"I don't think I've laughed as much in the past year as I have with you two," Erin observed. "I wish I didn't have to go back!"

"We'll be here when you return," Ruth assured her.

"Also, I'll be pestering you with phone calls every day, just like before," Allen added. "By the way, have you given my number to Stefanie in case of an emergency on your end?"

"Good point; I'll do it when I get back. You're one pest I will never call to have exterminated! I live for your calls, Sweet Talker," she smiled, gripping his hand.

She furnished her landline number as a backup for her cell. That was a comfort to him, because if her cell phone got lost or damaged, he had no other way to contact her previously. He would have had to wait for her to call.

She declared that unacceptable! Digging into her purse, she produced two business cards. On them were her phone numbers, address, email and social media accounts, as well as her company logo, A*C*E Video Productions. Beneath the name was printed "A Crushing Experience, made to order." They grinned as they read the words.

Erin chuckled, "Cheesy, I know, but I was going for something people would remember; besides, it's accurate, okay?" Allen never doubted that for a second!

They visited together until Ruth went to bed a little before eight. She said goodbye to Erin with a big hug, telling her welcome to the family, that she sure was enjoying getting to know her daughter-in-law to be! Erin said thanks, that she would be calling her, too. Ruth said she would be looking forward to it.

He had two hours before he had to leave for work. As they sat on the couch, she leaned toward him. They kissed, then she asked with a smile, "How are you at foot rubs?"

"I don't know," he said, "I've never given myself one."

Placing a throw pillow behind her, she turned crosswise, setting her feet in his lap.

"Would you mind?"

"Of course not," he grinned.

Her stylish boots extended maybe 6 inches above her ankles. He removed them, then asked about her socks, which she also wanted removed. Reaching down, she pulled her pant legs up to her knees as he began to knead the base of her toes and her soles. She sighed with pleasure, flexing her ankles slowly as he worked, assuring him he was doing it just right. He thought aloud that her feet were very pretty, admiring her high arches.

She grinned back at him, "I have a dirty little secret you should know."

"Tell you what," he bargained, "if you tell me yours, I'll tell you mine."

Now she was curious, "You have one, too?"

Using his thumbs to exert pressure as he rubbed her instep, he was rewarded with, "Ooooh, that's nice!"

"I do, but yours comes first."

"Okay," she said, "I dote on my feet. It goes beyond pedicures or painting my toes; I find myself playing with them whenever I don't have them covered. They're not ticklish, but for me, they are a serious erogenous zone. Affection shown them has an effect similar to kissing me, so you know; but rubbing and handling them as you are doing now makes me feel all warm and fuzzy inside.

"Something about it gets me feeling like if you are willing to stoop to show gentle attention to my feet, you must really care about me. I guess it's silly, but I wanted to share it with you, because it's personal. Is that weird?"

"Yes, that's really weird!" he responded, his hands recoiling as if burned. Her jaw dropped; a gasp of disappointment escaped her until she raised her eyes to spy his grin. He chuckled, but when he reached for her feet again, only air met his hands as she yanked them away. She wore a look of outrage as her feet beat a light tattoo of kicks against his thigh.

"That was mean!" she objected.

"I'm sorry; I couldn't resist giving you a hard time," he confessed, laughing.

A slightly harder kick with both feet followed on his thigh. "Meanie!" she said, but this time a smile broke through.

"I'm sorry," he repeated, "will you let me make it up to you, give me a second chance?"

"Okay, but I think you should apologize to them first," she said with a giggle. She held them up at face level; he did as she asked, giving each sole a kiss. She shuddered at each kiss, then stretched them out on his lap again. "You can rub them now; all is forgiven. They sure do like you, and they loved when you kissed them."

"Oh, they did, huh?"

He began to raise one to his lips, when it became heavy.

"You better not do that until after the wedding," she warned. "You would be amazed how forceful they can be when they get carried away."

"Oh! I didn't know."

She looked dignified as she leaned back to reiterate, "However, rubbing is welcome and highly encouraged."

He went back to a gentle massage, heard a sigh of contentment.

"I believe you also had a dirty little secret to share with me?"

CHAPTER 17

"Yeah, well, I'm having second thoughts about that," he admitted as he graduated to rubbing her ankles.

"Why?" she demanded.

"Well, I'm not sure if it's smart. I think you could make me do pretty much whatever you want already. Taking into account that we have established you are stronger than I am, it just doesn't seem to be a good idea to give you even more power over me. Does that make sense?"

Erin was inscrutable. "I have to say it does. You make a very good point. It's foolhardy to give away information that puts you at a disadvantage to someone else, unless you trust him or her completely."

"Well, I do trust you, at that," he thought aloud.

"Enough to keep your word to me and dish?" she challenged.

He saw something in her eyes he couldn't identify; he felt like she was measuring him.

"I did promise, didn't I?"

She silently nodded.

"Okay. I'm defenseless when it comes to you, anyway."

Her gaze softened. She wore a knowing little smile. "Go on," she prompted.

"I have a thing for your legs," he blurted out, turning red.

She grinned, seeming genuinely surprised, "Is that so?"

"The first time I saw you at the store counter with your back to me, it was the shape of them that caused me to notice you. Even in those ski pants, I could see their perfect proportions. I was hooked! You first noticed me when I approached the counter, but I was purposely scanning them from the side view.

"When you turned and noticed me, I glanced up to take in their owner. Our eyes met, which foiled my intent to admire your legs as you left. When I was checking out at the counter, I looked around, hoping to get one last glance at them as you left, hoping I wasn't too late. When you were standing there staring at me, you completely threw me off my game!"

She busted out laughing, "You horndog!"

He grinned sheepishly with a half shrug, "I'm a guy, what can I say?"

She reached out to take hold of his wrists, then guided his hands up to her calves. He gave a small involuntary gasp.

She said, "A foot rub isn't done until the calves are massaged, too; that's why I pulled my pant legs up. Think you're up for it?" she asked with amusement.

"Oh, wow!" was all he could say.

"Mmmmm," she said as he worked her taut muscles, "is that the whole story?"

"No," he said.

Her eyes widened.

"When we went to the pool, you exposed them to me for the first time when you came out of the bathroom wearing your bikini cover-up. I was mesmerized, thought I was going to have a heart attack! I couldn't take my eyes off your legs. I kept expecting you to see my fixation and make fun of me, but thankfully, you never did.

"That's when I realized how seeing you in swimwear would affect me. I decided to jump in the pool right away to try to salvage my dignity."

"How did I miss that?" she wondered. "I guess I wasn't paying attention."

"You were focused on showing off your bikini," he reminded her.

"Yes, I was. I wanted to make an impression on you. It didn't register that I already had," she giggled.

"You can stop, if you want," she motioned at his hands.

"Do I have to?" he asked.

She giggled. "No, you don't have to, but you're spoiling me at this point."

"I'm okay with that," he said.

With a smile she admitted, "Me, too."

They sat there for a bit as he continued to knead the length of her calves, even working down to her feet a couple of times, plainly appreciating her feminine perfection. She watched with a mix of amusement and satisfaction, flexing her legs, chuckling when he was startled at her movement.

"I had no idea my legs are your biggest turn-on. I'm gonna have fun with that knowledge now!" she announced with a wink.

He looked at her seriously, "Erin, I never said that."

Her confusion was plain to see. He explained, "So much about you makes my toes curl and gives me goosebumps; it's no wonder I'm crazy about you!

"Your features are breathtaking to me, from your long blonde locks that I can't help thinking of as a lioness' mane (never mind that there is no such thing), to the lovely little feet you just introduced to me so intimately. Your legs are spellbinding, but what I see doesn't turn me on as much as what you do."

Her full attention was on him, her eyes locked on his as he spoke. His hands went still, resting on the calf nearest to him. His eyes began to water.

"Sweet Erin, you touch me! I've always felt like something must be wrong with me that makes me untouchable. Maybe it's my reserve or the shyness I've never entirely been able to shake, but there's almost always a distance between me and others that seems untraversable, leaves me feeling alone, isolated – like maybe I'm not worth their effort!

"You reach for me; you touch me and hold me close. I matter to you! It comes across in the way you touch me, hold me, the way you let me hold you and hold your hand."

She reached down to take his right hand, held it firmly. Her eyes were moist, but a tear ran down his cheek.

"You want to know my biggest turn-on? Your hypnotic blue eyes are it, in a nutshell, because of the way you look at me. I utterly melt when I see the tender regard for me reflected in your gaze. It seems impossibly wonderful to see you look at me that way, not once, but over and over!"

Tears were running on both their cheeks now.

"My second biggest turn-on is your soft voice; not because it is appealing and pleasant, which it definitely is, but because it conveys a measure of the care you have for me. You turn me on in a million different ways, without even trying; but as long as you keep looking at me and speaking to me the way you do, I am yours and putty in your hands. Your lovely features, legs included, are just icing on the cake for me!"

Her legs swung down off his lap. She came up on one knee to drop into his arms, throwing her own around him.

Her kisses were intense; their tears mingled to soak both their faces, which got them laughing between kisses. She levered herself upward with her legs to push him over with her on top, then barraged him with kiss after kiss until he reminded her he was going to have to leave for work pretty soon.

"What if I won't let you up?" she teased.

"Then I'll just have to move you!" he declared.

It didn't happen, though. Every attempt he made to raise up or push her aside was countered, with minimal effort on her part. She rode out his struggles, entrenching herself atop him until her arms pinned his, while her legs locked his in a grip like a vise. She grinned above him like a cat that had just swallowed a canary.

"So when are you going to move me off of you?" she inquired.

"Maybe tomorrow, when you get ready to leave," he hazarded. "It obviously isn't going to happen tonight, unless you let me up."

"You're right about that," she laughed, then barraged him with kisses anew.

"Something tells me I better get used to you being on top," he observed.

She paused for just a moment, "You're learning!"

The kisses rained down all over his face as he turned his head uselessly, trying to avoid them.

"Hey!" he objected.

She continued, then laughed some more. "I'm *touching* you, Sweet Talker. Are you complaining?"

Opening his eyes, he looked directly into hers, "No way."

The next kiss came down squarely on his lips, deep and hungry. She stopped suddenly, moving off of him, "You better get ready for work, and I need to go. So, so tempting," she mumbled, as she reached for her socks and boots.

He sat up, taking a tissue to dry his face. She chuckled as she noticed.

He commented, "Very funny."

"*I* thought so," she responded. "Gives you something to think about at work, how much you're loved and wanted."

"Thanks for that, even if it was messy."

She giggled, "Anytime you want more, just let me know. I wonder if a guy can be drowned by too many kisses?"

His look brought more giggles.

"I was just wondering; can't fault a girl for being curious."

He chuckled, "What a way to go, smooched to death!"

They stood. She looked at him, shaking her head, "Smooched? Who says that? That's right up there with 'ornery'. You're turning out to be a living reference for last century terms, you know?"

His mouth dropped open; she caught his chin to close his mouth gently.

"The sad thing is that I don't have to look them up; I know what they mean. Guess that's just another indication that we're a match made in heaven, huh?"

"Literally," he replied as they walked out to her car, "and I stand by what I said before. You *are* ornery!"

They kissed twice, then she agreed with a sly grin, "Yes, I am, and proud of it!" They said goodnight, then he went in and prepared for work.

CHAPTER 18

As they agreed before, he met her at the motel when his shift ended the next morning. They had planned on having breakfast together before her departure, ending up at Village Inn. Not much was said; they were a bit melancholy about being parted.

He finally broke the silence, "You know, I've been thinking about what to call you."

"Huh?"

"Well, you seem to have settled on Sweet Talker as your pet name for me."

She grinned, "Yep. It's unique to you. No one talks to me as sweetly as you do and means it. I've had my share of flattery, can spot a con artist a mile away. Guys like that always have an angle, usually want sex or money."

"Commitment was more important to you than sex. It's just for you. You are my one and only Sweet Talker!"

He laughed. "I like that. I haven't addressed you by anything but your name. Babe, sweetheart, pretty lady, all those have been used on someone else. They have memories associated with them that have nothing to do with you. I wanted something unique for you, something that could only mean *you*. Do you mind if I call you Genie?"

"Why? Surely you don't think I'm going to address you as 'Master', do you?'

"Please don't, that would be embarrassing," he hurriedly replied. She smiled.

"Besides, I always thought Major Nelson was a bit of a dork." That got a laugh. "All that power at his disposal in a gorgeous woman who was determined to make him happy, yet all he could think about was how disruptive she was to his life. I like to think I'm smarter than that!"

"Some dogs are smarter than that," she observed. "Still, he married her. You haven't told me why you want to call me Genie."

"That's easy, Erin; you make my wish come true. I want to tell the world how you make my wish for happiness a reality, like magic!"

She gripped his hand, smiling broadly, "In that case, consider me your Genie and be careful what you wish for!"

"What does that mean?" It sounded vaguely alarming.

"It means you better not underestimate what I am capable of doing to and for you. I'm pretty sure I can blow your mind!" she raised her eyebrows.

He leaned over to kiss her, then admitted, "I bet you can, but I'm not worried. I'm in good hands."

She held on when he started to sit back, kissed him again. "I see what you mean about trust being sexy. When you relax to lower your guard with me, it makes me want to just eat you up! Don't worry, though; I'm committed to honor your beliefs. I'll keep my word and wait." She released him, then started playing with her ring.

"I never doubted that for a minute. When you come back, I hope you'll stay in the guest room. You won't take advantage of me. We have too much to lose; besides, you're way too shrewd for that. You didn't get where you are today without self-discipline. I trust you."

She laughed, "Who's shrewd? As competitive as I am, you just turned this into a challenge! Okay, I'll consider it, but I won't be the only one living with temptation, smart guy. You might as well know that I wear short shorts and a T-shirt to bed when I travel; think you can keep your hands to yourself?"

"Oh boy, what am I getting myself into?" he moaned, while she nodded, smiling. "Hey, I have an extra robe you can use while you're here."

"Maybe I'll make use of it, or maybe I won't," she teased. "Maybe I'll ask for a foot rub every night I'm here, after changing for bed. What do you think?"

"That's cruel!" he objected.

"I think the word you're looking for is 'ornery.' I've already admitted that I am," she chuckled. "I agreed to wait until we're married, but I never promised to make waiting easy for you! If it's not easy for me, why should it be for you?"

They bantered playfully over the meal until they finished and left the restaurant. When they kissed goodbye at her car, he took her left hand with his, bringing both up to view their rings.

"Goodbye is no fun, but August is coming closer every day," he reminded her, then kissed her hand tenderly.

"Yes, it is," she replied, her eyes watering. "I'm going to work myself clear of the day-to-day company routine as soon as I can, so I can be with you."

"I'll be waiting," he assured her. "I love you, Erin!" They kissed again and embraced, then she got in the car and he watched her go.

CHAPTER 19

They talked on the phone three times that day. Allen called her before going to bed that morning, just to hear her voice again. She said the love bug bit him good, which he conceded with a laugh.

The second time was when he got up, to check on her. She told him her cross-country drive that led to their meeting was a lark; she usually flew for long trips so as not to waste time, but she wanted some time alone to think. If not for that 'lark', they might have never met! The circumstances of their lives intersecting that day at the gas station continued to highlight the supernatural influence that made it so much more than just two ships passing in the night.

He was alert because long distance road trips were not routine for her. He was somewhat protective; it's a guy thing, he told her. Trucking was a prominent part of his resume; as a professional driver, he was well acquainted with the hazards of highway travel.

His concern for her was unnecessary, she assured him. It was nice to have someone so attentive to her well-being for a change, however, so if he wanted comfort by hearing her reassurance that she was okay, she didn't mind at all.

He took her word at face value, but got off the phone feeling self-conscious that he was doting on such an independent woman. Not wanting to offend, he resolved to put off calling her until tomorrow. He joked about being a pest but didn't want to be perceived as one.

She called him from Amarillo at 9:40 that night; she said she was checked into a motel. He thanked her for calling. They visited for a few minutes before she surprised him with news she had cracked open her new Bible. She started in Matthew, skipping the genealogy as he had recommended, but had one question. What did 'privily' mean?

He chuckled, saying dated English can be a bit odd at times, then explained it meant 'privately,' as opposed to publicly.

"Oh! Okay, Joseph didn't want to scandalize her for getting knocked up when he was thinking of breaking it off with her, I guess."

He couldn't help it; he cracked up laughing.

"What? Did I get it wrong?" she sounded defensive.

"No, Genie, you got it right. I do love you! I know you're looking into this because it matters to me. I would *never* poke fun at you for a labor of love! It's just that I've never heard the virgin birth referred to as being 'knocked up'. I know you're not being disrespectful; it just struck me as funny!

"You are exactly right in your understanding. At the time Joseph was considering breaking it off, he thought she was 'knocked up' and evidence of infidelity. What else could it be? If God didn't give him the dream explaining what really happened, he would have gone to his grave convinced she had cheated on him."

"Okay," she said, vindicated, "as long as you're not laughing at me. I don't mind telling you that you're wrong..., well, kind of wrong. I am reading the Bible because it matters to you, but there's more to it than that.

"I- I want to find out what God wants with me! Mom said you are His gift to me, to get my attention. He's got it now! If humans give away humans, that means someone is enslaved, but you're no slave. You have made it clear that's not something you would abide, even if it was what I wanted, which I don't."

"You're right about that. I would run away or kill myself before I'd live that way. Self-respect is too important to me; I couldn't stand to live without it. As much as I love you, it wouldn't be enough without your respect, and my own."

"I get that," she replied. "Only in the absence of love could someone ignore that need. You are a willing, living gift of God's provision, who put such love in my heart that the thought of hurting you is unbearable to me! I have made a career, even a good living dishing out pain to other men, yet He gives a particularly fragile, tender-hearted man to a man-breaker like me; doesn't He understand the risk He's taking?"

"There's no risk in the way He's done it, Erin. You just said it; you could only ignore my needs if I didn't matter to you. But he put that incredible affection in your heart for me, just like He placed it in mine for you! We wouldn't matter to each other without it. It comes from God, for God is love.

"I have no doubt either of us would take a bullet for the other. Self-sacrifice is the highest form of love, remember? It was modeled for us by Jesus on the cross; and my sweet Genie, He has seeded our hearts with that same care."

"Yeah, He has," she observed, "which is all the more reason to look into what He has to say, after all these years of dismissing Him over a foolish misunderstanding.

"I found out I'm not the first person God used dreams to reach, so that's encouraging. Chapter two said He gave a dream to the wise men and three to Joseph."

"Yep," he concurred, "of course, Stefanie would point out that even Joseph wasn't as hardheaded as you are."

She squawked, "I can't believe you went there! You're lucky I'm not with you, or you'd be in a side headlock right now!"

"I probably would," he said, laughing, "and I'd be laughing too hard to even try to do anything about it."

"You're no challenge at all," she snorted.

"I don't know about that," he rejoined. "Try not to smile when you're visiting with me."

She chuckled, "That's not a challenge, that's impossible." They enjoyed each other's company several more minutes before saying goodnight.

As his shift proceeded, his thoughts were full of the woman who had come to mean so much to him. He prayed for her soul, trusting that the Lord would set her free from sin. She said He had her attention now, but the world and the enemy that holds sway in it would work hard to distract her. If she did not come to Christ, the couple would eventually fall apart, because her love for him is supplied from His abundant stores; Allen knew he's not so lovable without Him.

She was unaware of the battle taking place in the heavenlies over her affections. She had no idea the opposition that would be coming her way; still, He who began this good work in her would be faithful to complete it, and He has overcome the world. She, too, was in good hands!

Her words linked up in his mind. He was no challenge at all, yet she would be disappointed if he didn't challenge her control in the bedroom, which she seemed to take for granted. Did she think he was such a pushover? Then again, he had no luck getting her off him on the couch, and he really had tried his best.

That was fun, but why was she so interested in physically contesting him? As he thought back to how she tossed him around in the pool (he still couldn't believe she was that strong), he realized she was simply showing off! Since no one else was there, it had to be for his benefit. The lifting contest in the weight room was another instance of the same thing. Proving her superiority by holding him down on the couch made three times.

In her words, "kissing him breathless" was to demonstrate her desire for him, not to show off; however, she certainly noticed that he couldn't prevent her, making sure to point it out to him. They spent four days together with four instances where her strength was underscored as surpassing his, not to mention all the verbal references relating to the same point. When she said she was competitive over breakfast, she was being modest!

He asked the Lord why it mattered so much to her to prove he was physically not her equal, also whether that question was motivated by wounded male pride. His thoughts turned to how he had accepted the newly discovered status quo without being indignant. None of it angered him at all, so pride was definitely not a factor.

As long as she didn't try to intimidate or publicly humiliate him, it would not be an issue. She had taken pains to reassure him that he would always be safe with her. It just took some getting used to, that he needed those reassurances!

After work the next morning, he ate, then got ready for bed before calling her, in case she was sleeping. He didn't have to wait; she was already on the road, making miles. They talked briefly. He warned her that reception tended to be spotty across New Mexico, so if they lost the call, it wasn't his doing. She said she wouldn't blame him then, just think of her. He chuckled, telling her he thought of little else!

She said, "Good boy! That's how it should be!"

They talked a bit longer until she started cutting out, then said goodbye. He went to bed.

CHAPTER 20

About 4:50 p.m. he woke feeling peaceful and lay still, praising God, thanking Him for His gifts and graciousness. A moment after he went silent, he heard Erin's voice stating very clearly, "My strength and my skills are what make me exceptional; otherwise, I'm just another girl."

He immediately responded, "Erin, that's not true! You have much more going…"

The sound of his own voice woke him. He sat up to look around. Erin wasn't there. It must have been a dream, but he could have sworn he heard her voice! *The Twilight Zone* theme went through his mind as he considered how real her voice had seemed.

He wondered aloud, "Lord, what was that?" She was hundreds of miles away. How could he hear her in his bedroom?

Trying to shake it off, he got around for the day. In front of the bathroom sink, a thought hit him; what if she really felt that way? That was enough to seek a second opinion, so he knocked on Ruth's door. After greetings were exchanged and a moment's visit, he shared the weird way he woke.

When he posed his question to her, she nodded, "Absolutely. We girls get a fixed idea of where our value or our talents lie; that gives us security. I don't have to tell *you* how important security is to us."

She didn't; he had decades of marital experience to fall back on, with biblical instruction underlying that. Women need love and security in a relationship, while men thrive on respect and affection. The world seems to come undone when these needs aren't met!

So, it clicked into place. Erin is trying to impress him with her abilities and strength, using his as the measure to prove hers. If she out powers him, it's not about one-upmanship; she just wants him to see how she excels! Like at the pool, where she was so intent on trying to impress him with her suit, she completely missed how she had already bowled him over with what he could see in her cover-up.

She couldn't wrap her mind around the idea that her shapely legs, natural extensions of her body, could be so enthralling to him, until he told her the effect they had on him. Since that required no effort on her part, she placed her efforts on feats to impress, her attention on gauging his response.

That describes guy behavior in courtship, but his girl was doing this with him! He asked God what he should do, thanking Him as it occurred that He had answered the question he had posed to Him last night. The thought came to mind, *Wrestle her*!

He was scandalized, immediately thinking God would never say that to him, it was completely improper. Was it really, though? The command resonated in him, echoed throughout his soul. No matter how extraordinary a man wrestling a woman was to him, he remembered it was routine for her. Would it mean something to her if he met her on the mats, where so much of her life was conducted?

Another thing to consider; she could mop the floor with him! She is a *pro*. There is no way he could realistically expect to win even a single match. Of this, he had no doubt at all! He was easygoing, but no one likes getting beat all the time. That could really take a toll on what ego he had left. He couldn't afford to lose his self-respect.

Talk to her about it; she will understand.

Okay. He trusted her with his most personal concerns to this point and she gave him no cause to regret it, so why not? Besides, if it turns out that she does enjoy hurting him in the heat of competition, maybe it's better to find out before they tie the knot!

After dinner, he called her. She had stopped for the night in Holbrook, Arizona, where she was getting checked into a motel. He offered to call her back, but she asked him to bear with her, so they talked as she conducted the transaction and entered her room. She apologized for the interruptions as she set the thermostat.

Settling into a chair, she explained that it had been a long day of driving. She was really missing him. Same here, he told her; well, the missing her, not the driving. She laughed, then asked how he slept. He had resolved not to tell her how he woke, which meant nothing as he spilled all of it! Why did he do that, he wondered?

When he repeated what he heard her voice speak in the bedroom, "My strength and my skills are what make me exceptional; otherwise, I'm just another girl," there was a distinct hesitation.

"You know I didn't say that," she stated unnecessarily.

"Erin, you weren't even here. I had to be dreaming, I guess. It just seemed so real. Before it happened, I woke up feeling a supernatural peace, which is a hallmark of the Lord's presence. I think the Lord is dealing with me about something He considers important."

"Weird! Well, I'm sorry my voice woke you up, even if it wasn't me talking," she chuckled, a little nervously.

He laughed, "Actually, it didn't. I woke up when I responded to your comment – well, what sounded like your comment."

"What did you say?" she asked sharply, to his surprise.

"Not much, sweetie. I told you it's not true, that you had much more – and I woke up to the sound of my own voice."

Hers had a quaver as she spoke, "Listen to me, Allen. I didn't say that!" There was a pause before she continued more quietly, "But I could have. It's accurate. What would you say in response? I *need* to hear it!"

"Erin, it's not true. Your strength and skills cause you to stand out, for sure, but you have so much more going for you than that! You are beautiful inside and out, generous to those not as blessed as you, while caring for others who will most likely never acknowledge how you were looking out for them. That's the kind of beauty no accumulation of years will ever obscure! If there is anything spiteful about you, I've yet to see it."

He could hear her crying, though it sounded like she was muffling her microphone. He did not stop.

"You are one of the smartest, most clever people I have ever met. You saw how others are turning a profit in your industry and said, 'I could do that,' then proved it! You haven't compromised by leaning on the crutches of sex or nudity that some of your competitors capitalized on, at the expense of their athletes. You adhered to higher standards, achieving success without sacrificing the integrity of those who trusted you."

"Okay, I get it," she laughed.

"Excuse me, but I wasn't finished," he went on. "You also have exquisite taste, which you exhibited in choosing me as your fiancé."

A burst of laughter punctuated the sniffling, "I can't argue with that."

Undeterred, he continued, "You are bold enough to bring me out of my shell and render me speechless, so unspeakably lovely as to reduce my considerable vocabulary to one three letter word, 'Wow,' and kind enough to hold an audience with me when it's less than convenient. If your strength deserted you tomorrow, if you forgot everything you knew about rendering an opponent helpless, I would still love you, would still be at your mercy. That is for you alone, unlike any other girl. Have I made my point?"

"Yes, sir. I won't be going there again," she giggled, still sniffling.

"Good! Bet you'll think twice about wanting to know what I was gonna say," he declared.

"Actually, no," she corrected him, "if anything, I am more determined than ever to draw you out, so I can hear you in full detail. If you're gonna tell me how wonderful you think I am, I want to hear it! Who am I to let your self-expression be stifled? Artistic growth should always be encouraged," she finished.

"You didn't learn a thing from all that, did you?" he snorted.

"Sure I did," she rejoined, "I learned that whatever you leave off saying is worth having you complete the thought, even if I have to twist your arm to get it out of you. Believe me, I'm just the woman to do it, if need be!"

"That's not nice!" he objected.

"No, it's not," she said sadly, "I guess it's … ornery!"

He moaned aloud while she laughed.

"Seriously, do you have any idea what He's dealing with you about, since it seems to be about me?" she inquired.

"I think He is trying to give me insight about what matters to you," he replied. "I will sound it off you the next time we see each other."

"Oh." He could hear her disappointment.

"It'll keep," he told her. "I really need to see your reaction for myself. Besides, you can't twist my arm until then, anyway."

"It sounds like there won't be a need to." A few minutes later they said goodnight.

CHAPTER 21

T he next morning, she called him, ten minutes after his shift ended. After a cheerful greeting, she said that she was eating breakfast while reading Matthew chapter three.

"I have a question," she said. "If Jesus was perfect and never sinned, why did He ask John the Baptist to baptize Him? I thought He had no sin to repent of, which is the whole point of baptism, isn't it?"

"That's a very insightful question, Genie. Most folks never think to ask about it. They just think John's objection was simply a deferral to Christ, as a properly humble man.

"Jesus had no need to repent of His sins because He had none. He is the only begotten Son of Father God, but He is also the offspring of a human mother with a heritage of sin. With that blended heritage, it was only right that He display a humble attitude toward the Father He desired to honor.

"It was a personal expression, but the public display of baptism set an unmistakable example for all who would come to Him. It also endorsed John's ministry in the process."

"That makes sense. If it was a personal gesture to His Father, it explains the extravagant response of seeing the heavens opened and the Spirit descending on Him like a dove."

"You *have* asked Him to explain things to you, haven't you?" It was more a statement than a question.

"Yeah, I have. Mom said I should!"

"Genie, I'm just blown away by your comprehension of what you are reading! Many professing Christians don't have the grasp of scripture you are showing me. Even as smart as you are, well, let's just say He is answering your prayer already!"

"Well, that's good to know," she said. "It's not hard to understand, so far. Can you tell me what made John's baptism so special? Israel flocked to the guy in the boonies, even though he dressed like a caveman and ate bugs. I would have written him off as a nutcase!"

Allen laughed, "As a Gentile like me, any of us would have at that time. He meant nothing to the Roman occupation; but to a Jew living under the Law of Moses, his message was revolutionary!

"The Law taught that for sins to be forgiven, animal sacrifices must be offered up in the Temple by the priests, following specific instructions. The Jew's penitence was evidenced by his confession of sin with the provision of the animal to be sacrificed. It was humbling to go public with your transgression, not to mention costly! Many people couldn't afford it, so it was assumed that God rejected them.

"Then John shows up from the backside of the desert with a brand-new message. He says the long-awaited Messiah is coming, the Lamb of God appointed to die for the sins of the whole world. All you had to do now was confess your sins, repent, and God would provide the sacrifice once for all! Repent and trust God, who would justify you by your faith in His word.

"It made heaven accessible to even the poverty-stricken! Anyone receiving the message could be baptized. It might have sounded like a pie in the sky promise, but when John saw Jesus and identified Him as the Lamb of God promised in scripture -"

"Oh! I see what you mean! That would make for a very exciting time to be alive," she concluded.

"Uh-huh, but a dangerous time, too. The priesthood had become corrupt. They saw the Temple sacrifices as their livelihood. If God provided one sacrifice for all sin, they feared they would be hungry and out of work! Bet you can see the clash coming over that!"

"Okay, this is getting interesting, but I have to get on the road. Thank you for explaining things for me."

"Erin, there is no one I enjoy visiting with more than you, certainly no one I'd rather talk about than Christ! I am honored by your questions and trust."

"Sweet Talker, I love you! There's nothing phony about your take on religion, or I would have no patience with it. If it hadn't been for my dreams, I probably still wouldn't hear you out; but they and you have changed things for me.

"You are answering my questions, but you are not preaching to me or trying to change me. I respect that. You haven't condemned me for not believing as you do; you even make me feel good about myself when I'm out of my depth. I can't tell you how I appreciate that you don't talk down to me!"

"I wouldn't dare!"

She started laughing.

"You promised not to hurt me, but I can't imagine how provoking you would be a healthy choice!"

She was laughing hard. "But that's not why you respect me, goofball!"

"No, I respect you because you deserve it, but where is the drama in admitting that?"

A fresh outburst of mirth answered his inquiry.

"Great! Now you've got me giggling as I'm about to get on the road. Everyone that sees me laughing at nothing will think I've lost my mind!"

He chuckled, "*Or*, they might think, there goes one happy lady, maybe she's getting married."

"They'd be right, then," she noted.

"Yes, they would. If you catch someone giving you an odd look while you're smiling or giggling, show them your ring, point to it, then grin some more. They'll get it and grin back!"

"That will be fun! I'll do that!"

"I love you, Genie. You bring joy to my life! Be careful on the road, 'kay?"

"I will," she promised. "Talk to you in a while. 'Bye!"

She called him after dinner from Barstow, California, to tell him she had settled for the night. Almost immediately, she wanted to know if everything was okay. He assured her it was. Why did she ask?

"I had this feeling all afternoon that something was wrong. I could have gone further, but I couldn't shake it. I really wanted to talk to you without having to worry about losing the connection. Women's intuition is a real thing, Allen! I've learned over the years not to ignore it. How are you doing?"

"Aww, Genie, I wouldn't have bothered you with my moods," he said. "Your call this morning put a smile on my face going to bed. I slept well, then got up with the idea of getting a haircut, so I did. I'm sure you noticed it's getting thin up top."

"Yeah, I noticed. It's not unusual among guys your age. It doesn't matter to me. Does it bug you?" she inquired.

"A little," he confessed. "I discussed changing the style with the barber. We talked about a crew cut, but he doesn't think it's warranted yet. I commented that I never thought my hair would divorce me; it was bad enough when she did. He thought it was funny. That's what I was going for when I said it, but I've been in a funk ever since. It depressed me, the more I thought about it. Sometimes my failures catch up to me, you know?"

"Allen, listen to me. What's done is done, so leave it in the past. Quit blaming yourself for how things worked out! She made the decision to file against you, so there's no way it was all on you. God knew she would; that's why He started lining things up for you and me. If you were still married when we met, would our relationship or our plans exist today?"

"No, we wouldn't even know each other."

"That's right," she confirmed, "so leave it in the past, where it belongs. I am thrilled to be planning a future with you; I hope you are, too!"

"You can't know how much you mean to me, Erin! You don't think my screwed-up emotions make me damaged goods?"

"Not in the slightest," she answered instantly. "You are grieving the loss of a thirty-eight-year relationship. That's normal. You aren't damaged goods, you're just human! A lot of memories are associated with what you have lost. It's not reasonable to think you can just forget all that! Besides, you shouldn't forget everything; surely some of those are good memories. But that is all they are, Sweet Talker, memories!

"We have a lifetime of history behind us, without which we wouldn't be who we are today. I understand that someone you trusted rejected you, left you wounded. But

God Himself brought you someone else to love you more than life itself! Do I need to hold you down and cover you with kisses again to remind you of that fact?"

"No," he laughed, "that memory is still very fresh."

"I hope so," she chuckled. "Be advised that more such memories are in your future! You and I don't have anywhere near thirty-eight years' worth of memories to reflect back on yet, but we've made a few. Focus on them, okay? No one can change the past, so leave it behind. Think of the future we will make together, because *that* is the reality we are facing now!"

"How did you become so wise?" he marveled.

She laughed, "Women know what their guys need; it's in our genes. Listen to your barber – you don't have to resort to a crew cut yet! I'll let you know if that becomes appropriate, understand?"

"What, so now you think that's your decision to make?" he demanded.

"Not entirely," she admitted reasonably, "but I do think I deserve to have some input. You don't have to agree with me, but at least discuss it first. My opinion ought to matter that much!"

"Okay, that's fair. I wonder, though, if I would get the same consideration if you decided to change your hairstyle."

"Not at all," she quipped. "You would see it after I did it. That is a woman's prerogative!"

"That's not fair! Doesn't my opinion matter to you?"

"More than you know!" she said, "I'll make sure to get it, after I make the change." There was silence for a moment, then he heard her giggle.

He relented, "I can't imagine you making a change I don't like, anyway."

She followed up, "I can't feature you being so dumb as to tell me you don't like the change I make. You're way too shrewd to make that mistake," she stated with a laugh.

"Who's shrewd?" he rejoined. "I think I just received a warning disguised as a compliment, or was it a threat?"

"No threat was intended or implied," she clarified, "just a reminder that there are consequences for every choice, including one's choice of words. I am confident that you are mindful enough of your words to keep out of trouble, for the most part," she finished smugly.

He paused, "You're a little scary sometimes, you know that?"

She cracked up laughing.

"Thank you for not getting hurt or offended at my issue, Erin. Also, thank you for making room in your life for me. Until you came into mine, I thought it had become nothing more than a test of endurance without joy. I felt so alone."

"You are not alone anymore, Sweet Talker. You never will be again. I'm here for you, a phone call away, if not closer still. You are every bit as much a comfort to me as I try to be for you. I love you with all my heart," she concluded.

"I love you too, Genie. Talk to you soon."

CHAPTER 22

About 9:30 p.m. she called again.

"Hey, twice in one evening!" he laughed.

"I'm missing you, so I didn't need much of an excuse," she said, "but I do have one. I read chapters four and five of Matthew. Chapter five is kind of overwhelming. Jesus said to cut off your hand and pluck out your eye? You haven't, obviously, nor have I seen one Christian who has. If a guy looks at a woman and wants her, He says the guy has already committed adultery, even though he hasn't touched her at all! Who can live like this? Who would want to? Am I missing something here?"

"As Gentiles, we don't have the background knowledge of the Law of Moses that His listeners had; that's what is missing. We were never expected to live by it, like they were. Verse twenty is key to understanding the chapter, 'Except your righteousness exceed that of the scribes and Pharisees, you will not enter the kingdom of heaven,'.

"The Temple scribes taught that God would be pleased by keeping the letter of the Law; you know, do this and this, but don't do that. The Pharisees epitomized the fine details of religious observance in practice. No one made a show of keeping the rules of the Law better than they did.

"The problem was, they were phonies! They seemed to keep the Law publicly, but their hearts were unchanged, wicked. Living by a rule book doesn't teach anyone to love God, which is the very first of the Ten Commandments!

"Love changes everything: how one views God, his neighbors, even his enemies. Loving God is the motivation for hating and rejecting sin, because these things separate us from Him. The people He was addressing had repented of their sins at John's teaching, were glad to be baptized; however, self-righteous hypocrites believed that their deeds justified them, so they saw no reason to repent.

"Therefore, Jesus declared His repentant audience to be the light of the world and the salt of the earth, rather than the outwardly holy but inwardly corrupt religious fanatics of the day. He pointed out that sinful desires in the heart would eventually work their way out to become sinful deeds that destine people to hell. It would be better to pluck out the lustful eye, to cut off the hand that reaches for what it should never touch, before committing sin that results in judgment. Is this making sense?"

"I think so. Jesus was calling out overly religious people who thought they could trick God, but never really cared about Him."

"Exactly! He quoted one of the prophets to put it in a nutshell, 'These people worship Me with their lips, but their hearts are far from Me.' He instructed His listeners to love their enemies because the Father in heaven shows kindness and grace to those who hate Him. It honors our heavenly Father when we act like He does; besides, we never want to put ourselves in a position where we have to justify what we have done to someone else. God will judge hypocrites for that very thing!"

"Then our lustful thoughts and desires don't cause an issue with God? Or do they?"

"Erin, lust is the initial impulse that draws couples together; otherwise, why would we be interested in pursuing one another? God built our desire into us for that reason, so we would comfort each other and bear children.

"We *are* expected to control our lusts, not let them control us. Jesus' use of the term 'adultery' implies that the one being lusted after is another man's wife, therefore off-limits. Adultery is also forbidden in the Ten Commandments, leaving no question that it is sin."

"So, my desire for you is not sin, right?" she posed.

"No more than mine for you, Genie. He knows how we feel about each other. He brought us together knowing in advance the chemistry we would have, the temptation we would face and the choices we would make in establishing a relationship free of shame. He *smiles* when He sees how we are conducting ourselves. When the time arrives for us to consummate our marriage, He will be just as pleased as we are."

"Hmm." he could hear her mulling things over, "Sex pleasing God; it's not something I've ever considered. I guess I thought that if He is real, He must be a total prude."

"He created both genders, so He effectively invented sex," Allen extrapolated. "I don't think a prude would think like that! Amoebas are asexual and He created them, too, so if sex acts offended Him, He could have created us differently.

"He made us to be His companions. As a spiritual being, He is capable of an intimacy flesh and blood humans cannot even grasp; but sex gives us the barest hint of what it must be like, momentarily. Imagine what it would be like to be fulfilled, complete, perfect all the time, unable to experience loneliness!"

"I can't imagine that! It sounds unbelievable. How do you know He intends that for us?"

"From how He ends the chapter, 'Be ye therefore perfect, as your Father in heaven is perfect.' If that statement is a command, is it reasonable?"

She chuckled, "Nobody is perfect; surely He knows that."

"Yes, He does. However, if it's a wish for us, like 'Have a nice day,' it takes on another meaning. When the Creator of the universe says it, it becomes more than a wish; it becomes a verbal revelation of His plan for anyone willing to agree to it!"

"Oh, wow! Is that even possible?"

"With God, all things are possible; Jesus taught us that. The only thing preventing it is sin, so He is on His way to the cross to take care of *that* personally."

She caught her breath, "Why wouldn't everyone sign on to His plan, then?"

He heaved a sigh, "I hope I don't offend you, Genie, but you haven't."

Dead silence greeted him as he continued, "You are still evaluating what He has to say, looking to see what it will cost you; at least you are giving Him a chance.

"Not everyone believes Him, that He is as good as He says or that we are as bad as He says we are. Some are offended at being called evil; folks like that crucified Him. Others tune Him out, preferring something more pleasant to their ears.

"When He urges us to take up our cross to follow Him, it indicates that we must be willing to lay down our lives for Him as He did for us. Many consider that cost too high, so they are unwilling to make Him the top priority in their lives. I guess priorities are what it comes down to, in the final decision.

"Have I overstepped with you? I'm only trying to be honest in answering your questions."

A long pause ensued, "If I didn't love you so much, Allen, this conversation would be over, and you would never see me again; but I can't just shoot the messenger! You *are* just responding to what I ask. Your honesty is brutal without intending to be. I can't help but respect you for it. You don't scare me in the slightest, but He does! When you represent Him to me, it's like I'm facing Him, not you, if that makes sense."

"It does," he replied. "He came into my heart to live in me by my invitation. He sometimes speaks through me; He is making me more like Him as time goes by."

"I can tell," she said slowly. "Earlier this evening, you were fighting depression, you needed my comfort; but now, you have an iron edge, knowing exactly where you stand, what you believe. You are a contradiction in terms I am finding hard to reconcile, my Sweet Talker. You say I am faced with two people, the one I love and Christ living in you – which means I'm engaged to both!"

He couldn't help but laugh. "I'm sorry," He apologized, "I just never thought of it that way."

"I'm beginning to realize I can't have one without the other. It's a lot to take in," she concluded seriously.

"Erin, you are seeing things exactly as they are because He is giving you insight. As much as I love you, He loves you even more! You wouldn't want me without Him; that's not humility talking, either. He is what is good in me; otherwise, I am capable of great evil. He drew me to Himself, is still reshaping me into His likeness.

"You could have Him without me, but He saw what a blessing we could be to each other, so He brought us together against all probability, filling our hearts with this intense love we still can't explain. I suspect He is walking a fine line with you; that if it were not for your love for me, you wouldn't give Him the time of day!"

She broke out laughing; it sounded strained. "You got it! For better or worse, you are the reason I'm listening to Him at all, Sweet Talker. You are the bait He is using to lure me into the trap. I know this, but I don't care! I want you that badly! I think it's entirely possible that I would sell out to Him, in order to have you!

"My head tells me I should run for my life, but my heart aches at the thought of going on without you. Then I talk with you; somehow, it makes everything right again. The dreams of you made me crazy, but the reality makes me feel at war with myself. I didn't even know this, but our conversation seems to be congealing the truth for me.

"He scares me, but I can't stand the thought of losing you; however, it is becoming clear to me that you two are a package deal! Will it always be like this?"

"No. As soon as you decide to receive or reject Him, that battle is over, Genie. When you receive Him, our plans will go forward, and you will realize the potential of all those dreams you had. If you were to reject Him, I would lose my appeal to you; you would soon wonder what you ever saw in me."

"Impossible!" she cut in, "I love you! I always will!"

"That love is yours because you took it to heart as your own, my sweet girl, but it isn't natural. You loved me before you met me. How is that natural? Your love is a fragment, just a splinter of His boundless love for me. Were you to reject Him, your decision would eject the love for me that He has shared with you. You would move on quickly."

"I could never do that!" she objected.

"May I make an observation and offer an opinion that might simplify things for you?" he offered.

"Please do," she almost pleaded. The desperation in her voice was plain.

"I don't think the Lord really scares you the way you think. You are used to being in control; you like it that way. Maybe you are convinced you need to be in control to make sure things work out like you want. As an orphan who grew up with very little control of your life, who could fault you for wanting to make the world stop spinning around you? The best way to do that was to lock it down with an iron grip.

"Your lifestyle reflects that outlook. You take down big, strong guys, forcing them to submit to you repeatedly, reinforcing the idea that you have complete dominion in your life. It reassures you, builds your confidence, while shielding you from failure.

"When someone overcomes you, you determine to hone your skills to a razor's edge. It's more than being competitive; it is a *determination* that you will not be beaten again. That drive is what pushed you to become one of the best wrestlers in the world.

"Now you find yourself in my position, when it comes to Christ Jesus. I know my new partner is stronger than I am; likewise, you have become aware that He is stronger than you will ever be. I am at peace with what I've learned because I trust you, so I don't have to be in control.

"You don't have that peace because you don't know Him. Add to that the devil's whispers that Jesus will force you into choices against your will and strong-arm you, because He can; isn't that what stronger opponents do? I think you fear the Lord will dominate you, if you say yes to Him."

Allen took a deep breath, deliberately giving her time to deny what he said.

She made no sound, so he went on, "However, the devil's lie is becoming ever more evident. Your choices continue to be your own. God gave you dreams about me, but it was your decision to share them, to make yourself known to me. If you hadn't, all I would know is that you were a pretty woman I saw once with great legs!"

She cracked up laughing, "You are so funny!"

"I'm just telling the truth. I wanted to stay in touch, but you wanted more than that. God shaped your dreams of being with me, but you pursued me. I had no strength to go after you; you saw that and came after me wholeheartedly. I never had a chance!"

She giggled like a schoolgirl.

"For the record, I'm very glad you did. Then I gave you a Bible, but you decided to look into it. Now you are learning about Christ and feeling small. He has that effect on everyone, by the way, but the decision of what to do with Him is still entirely yours!

"Your choices will remain your own, because He is a gentleman. He will express His love for you, but He chooses not to force His way on anyone. He tempers His boundless strength with boundless tenderness, similar to how you choose to show me tenderness, rather than turn me into a pretzel!

"Fear of what you can do to me could cause me to retreat from you, but you say you love me. I believe you. You tell me you won't hurt me; I accept your promise, take you at your word. Your embrace holds no fear for me, because I choose to trust you.

"You are just becoming acquainted with the Lord. The time will come when He will ask you, 'Do you trust Me?'

"You will look back, remembering that all He ever did was offer you gifts, first me, then Himself. You will recall how I gave you my trust in spite of my vulnerability. The memory will challenge you, and I know my Genie will rise to the challenge, because she doesn't back down! The choice is yours to make, when you're ready. Does any of that help?"

"You have your mom's gift for putting things in perspective, Sweet Talker. If I am not losing control over my own choices, then there's no risk in going further. I can do that, with you by my side. I may wield the strength in this relationship, but you are the heart that makes it come alive!"

"Much of what you love about me is actually what you see of the Lord in me, Erin. You're gonna realize at some point that you know Him better than you think you do; when that happens, your fears will dissolve into joy and laughter!"

She seemed to relax. They talked a bit more, then said goodbye so he could go to work.

CHAPTER 23

They visited the next morning as his day ended and hers began. She told him the sound of his voice was infinitely better than the fading memories of the dreams he once inhabited to start her day.

He said that was nice to hear. Her voice was always a comfort to him. She chuckled when he reminded her it was also his second biggest turn-on.

She asked if it affected his dreams, to which he responded, "No comment." When she wanted to know why, he explained that if he said yes, she would want him to share the dreams with her. Rehashing such things would keep him awake, when he needed his sleep, okay? Mercifully, she let it go with a mischievous laugh.

She arrived home in the afternoon. With her girls present, clients coming and going, and the occasional guest wrestler there to record sessions, the place stayed busy during the week. Of course, Stefanie was a constant presence overseeing everything taking place. In the hustle and bustle, Erin's appearance would scarcely be noteworthy, most of the time; but a pretty gold ring on her left hand made an event of it!

The word spread like wildfire, until more than twenty people were congregating to see for themselves. She reluctantly met them in the oversized reception area to explain. Even the customers who knew Erin would take an interest in the news; she had a devoted fan base. Stefanie gathered nearly everyone in the house for Erin's announcement.

When it was made, a rousing cheer went up from the crowd! Erin recounted how she had been planning retirement for some time. That was not news to anyone there; however, with a new life to plan and someone to share it, her departures would be more frequent and of increasingly longer duration, until the company would be left entirely in Stefanie's hands.

Stef told her on behalf of all present how thrilled they were that she had found happiness, but she would certainly be missed. A number of faces teared up as heads nodded in agreement. Some of those present went back to what they were doing, particularly matches that had been interrupted.

Erin answered questions, also showing a picture of Allen on her cell phone to all wanting to see what he looked like. The inevitable request to know how they met was a story that didn't make sense until she made her dreams public knowledge. The crowd was spellbound as she laid it out, leading up to the meeting at the little store in Springfield, Missouri, and the initial visit with Allen that followed.

She realized the explanation of her dreams was likely to result in a flood of new questions, so she suspended the tale at that point, promising to post more details on her website soon. Citing that many who would be interested in the news were not present, it was only fair they should be informed, too; besides, she would rather not have to repeat it endlessly. The gathering slowly dispersed, with Erin getting hugs or handshakes from well-wishers in the process.

When it was over, she took a deep breath and sank into a chair. Stef clapped her on the shoulder with a half-smile, "Which was more exhausting, the travel or the arrival, sister?"

Erin grinned, "The road was restful, compared to this!"

Stef replied, "Well, catch your breath and call your man so he won't worry. I need to see the day wrapped up, but you know I will want to be brought up to date this evening!"

As she was about to leave the room, she stopped to reach for Erin's left hand. Admiring the ring, she said, "It is beautiful! It really looks good on you. You are practically glowing! It delights me to see you so happy. Welcome back!"

She walked off without waiting for a reply, leaving Erin reflecting on her words. The grin returned as she realized she truly was happy. Her smile did not fade as she called to notify Allen that she was back safe.

After dinner with Stefanie, Erin found herself sitting in front of her computer, intending to post news of her engagement on her website. The problem was that so much had transpired, she was drawing a blank as to how to get started.

The subject of God was touchy, too. It couldn't be avoided in explaining the dreams; yet without the dreams as foundational to meeting Allen, she would come off sounding like a mindless giddy girl who inexplicably fell for a yokel she had never seen before! That was not at all acceptable! She had her pride; besides, she already mentioned the dreams to those present earlier, and they would talk.

She didn't feel qualified to present a case for God. She wasn't sure enough of Him to commit herself to believing in Him, yet. It could be presented as Allen's take on things, but that was kind of cowardly, to her way of thinking. If opinions were voiced that were derogatory of him, she would be incensed; but without a clear-cut perspective of her own, any defense she offered for him would only appear to be emotionally based.

She wasn't about to feed him to the wolves without standing beside him! Any way she broke it down, she needed to decide where she stood on this matter. Her ability to stand with her love hinged on it, both now and in the future!

Turning off her computer, she broke out her Bible, then got comfortable to read. Before she opened it, she closed her eyes and spoke uncertainly, "God, it's me, Erin, if You're there. I'm not sure I believe in You, but Allen and Mom do, and they're not fools. Mom said to ask You to help me understand this book. Allen says my comprehension shows You are doing it.

"If You are real, I need to know for sure, so I'm going to dive into this over the weekend and try to settle the question. Would You help me?"

Gentle warmth settled over her; it seemed to comfort her. The uncertainty as she spoke into the air dropped away.

"One more thing, God – Jesus. If Allen is really your gift to me," the tears began to roll as she broke down crying, "I can never thank You enough! I have never loved *anyone* this much, or ever felt so loved in my whole life! If You care so much for me, I *will* spend the rest of it living for You; just show me You are real, that it's all true!"

The warmth persisted as she blew her nose and dried her eyes, then opened the book in her lap.

CHAPTER 24

A little before midnight, Allen got a call. "Hi, Sweet Talker. Is it okay that I called this late?"

Erin's voice was always welcome, and he told her so; he could afford a few minutes. "What's up?" he asked.

"Well, I'm wondering what kind of treasures can be laid up in heaven. You know what they say, you can't take it with you, so what does Jesus mean when He tells us to lay up treasures in heaven?"

"Oh, you're doing a little late-night Bible study, huh?"

"Yes, I am. I have decided to use this weekend to make up my mind about God, once and for all. If He is so important to you, I need to settle it to stand with you. I'll be the pest calling you for a change with lots of questions; I hope that's okay."

"I love it! You are never a pest to me, Erin, not even when you're covering my face with kisses."

She chuckled, "You're sure about that? 'Cause more is coming!"

He laughed, "Years ago, there was a commercial for Eggo waffles. A little boy and his big sister had grabbed the waffle in the toaster, saying, 'Leggo my Eggo!' She warned little brother that if he didn't let go, she was gonna kiss his whole face! He recoiled and let her take it, saying 'Eeewww!'."

"I think I remember that," she chuckled.

"I wondered how she would do that. Her mouth wasn't that big," he said.

Erin laughed. Her laughing continued as he informed her, "You educated me. Now I know what she meant!"

"Glad I could teach you something," she came back. "Who says you can't teach an old dog new tricks?"

"Ouch! That wasn't nice," he reproached her, just getting another laugh.

"To answer your question, I'll quote the Apostle Paul, 'Christ died for sinners, of whom I am chief.' Jesus treasures people, Erin. He endured the cross for us. He gave us the gospel of salvation so we could direct folks to Him, that they might be saved. When they go to heaven, they are the treasures attributed to us by our testimony. This world's money means nothing in heaven, but the family of Christ means everything to Him!"

"And people are not eaten by moths or susceptible to rust. Of course!" she finished. "That makes sense. Thank you!"

She thought a moment, "So if I accept Christ, I'll be your treasure in heaven?"

"Genie, you are my perfect treasure. I get to rejoice over you here in this life and in heaven both, should you choose Him. What could ever be better?"

"I miss you, Sweet Talker. I wish I could put my arms around you and hold you right now. You make me feel so wonderful!"

"You are wonderful, even if you did just liken me to an old dog," he responded. "Maybe that's what I am to you, a loyal old dog you are taking pity on."

Laughter gave way to an indignant snort, "I wouldn't marry anyone out of pity! Now you're lucky I'm not there!"

"Let me guess," he filled in, "I'd be back in that side headlock again?"

"How can anyone be so…?" she stalled, frustrated.

"Ornery?" he offered helpfully.

Both of them cracked up together in a moment of shared joy, then said their goodbyes.

"Good morning," Allen answered her call, about 8:15 the next morning.

"Hi, lover! I have another question. Oh, did your shift go okay?"

"Yeah, thanks for asking. What have you got?"

"Jesus said to enter by the strait gate; I'm sure He meant heaven. What is the 'strait gate'?"

"That is Jesus Himself, Genie. A lot of people think Christianity is about Christ, but it's not. Faith leads us directly to Christ. It is an encounter, a confrontation with Him personally, without which one will never enter heaven! He calls Himself the door and the gate to the sheep later on. He is one Man, so only one person at a time can enter a gate that size. That makes it very personal for whoever He allows in!"

"Whoa! That means if someone knows about Christ, attends church and even lives like a Christian, he can still go to hell?"

"Exactly," he agreed, "Jesus said His response will be 'I never knew you.' That's not something He could say to anyone who entered by the strait gate and had that personal interaction with Him."

She let out a low whistle. "He said many would go by the way of destruction. Are they just playing church and pretending to follow Him?"

"Some are," he qualified, "but many are deceived. They were told, often in a church, that if they repeated a short prayer after the minister, they were assured a place in heaven. A few scriptures were referenced to back up the claim. The scriptures are true, but God knows every heart.

"Some are just mouthing words that mean nothing to them. Some are riding a wave of emotion; as soon as their mood changes, their priorities shift. Jesus will present His parable of the sower a few chapters later that details these things. A personal encounter with Him is life-changing for whoever accepts Him; however, any who think they can accept what they like about Him and discard what they don't like are fooling themselves all the way to hell!"

"That is serious business!" she thought aloud.

"So was the cross, Genie. Jesus died the most painful death known to man to save us, so He wasn't playing around! Hypocrites insult His sacrifice, ultimately fooling only themselves. They incite ridicule from unbelievers, who should be moved by how we care for each other to wonder why we do; instead, turning them cold to the very gospel which could save their souls!

"If Jesus were dead, He would be rolling over in His grave; but since He is alive, He will hold accountable every person whose conduct has worked to nullify the effectiveness of what He accomplished at the cross! That's why the Bible warns that judgment begins in the house of God!"

"Then sinners are better off than hypocrites when facing Him," she stated quietly.

"He won't be as angry with them, but they all still end up in hell," he replied. "If parts of it are hotter than others, it's still not a good outcome or a happy place. The worst thing is that none of them had to go there. They will be acutely aware that if they had believed Christ, confessed and repented of their sins, they never would have seen that awful place! Can you imagine the regret they will feel? Jesus said there will be weeping and gnashing of teeth for the choices they made!"

"And you're worried that if I somehow died today, that's where I'd be headed?"

A sob rose in him, but he choked it off, mostly. An odd noise still preceded his response, "You would be. And you would break my heart when you left."

She took a deep breath before saying boisterously, "Well, I'm not dead yet and I'm looking into these things, so cheer up already! I *like* the idea of being your treasure, mister! You don't get rid of me that easily. If God is talking to me, He'll get His point across this weekend; if He doesn't, then He has nothing to say! Doesn't He finish what He starts?"

"Yes, ma'am, He does!" Allen couldn't help grinning. "He wouldn't dare refuse your challenge. Thank you for keeping me in the loop while you're wrestling with Him. Just remember this: if you win, you lose, but if He wins, you both win. This is not like any match you've ever had before!"

"I heard that," she agreed, "though I'm not sure what you mean about the conditions for winning."

"That's okay," he told her, "just know that Mom and I are praying for you. I'm here whenever you need me. I love you!"

Just above a whisper he heard her, "I know. It's what is keeping me going. I love you, Sweet Talker. I'll be in touch," then she hung up.

CHAPTER 25

When he woke for the restroom, there was a text from Erin, "Call me when you wake." He did, assuring her he didn't mind; he knew what she was doing was vital.

"What did He mean, the kingdom of heaven suffers violence and the violent take it by force? I thought heaven is supposed to be peaceful, not dangerous!"

He chuckled, "You're right, Genie, people will be safe there. Look at the time frame – from John the Baptist until now, when Christ was on His way to the cross. John taught the people to repent and trust God to provide the sacrifice for their sins. Those who obeyed were immediately justified by their faith, even though the sacrifice was yet to be offered up; yet the Law indicated there is no forgiveness of sins without the shedding of blood.

"However, God sent John to preach repentance, so He couldn't turn away those who did. Their faith forced God to accept them before Christ's sacrifice at the cross! His blood at the cross was applied to their sins retroactively from the time they repented. Does that make sense?"

"Kind of like an advance tax refund paid out at the time of filing, then. It seems remarkable at the time, but doesn't change things in the long run," she noted.

"You got it! No one had ever forced God's hand before that time. Faith in God's word preached by John put God's faithfulness to the test for a time, unintentionally. Jesus found it remarkable enough to put mention of it into scripture, because once again the Father's faithfulness was shown to be without fault, perfect. He never allowed an opportunity to glorify His Father to go by without responding."

"Okay, thanks. I'll let you get back to sleep. Sweet dreams!"

About 1:30 p.m. another text came. He was sleeping light enough it woke him. It read "Me again ???" He called Erin.

She greeted him, "That was quick. Did I wake you?"

"Yes, but you're worth it," he told her.

"Aawww, you're gonna get kissed for that when I see you! I have a question."

"Again?" he laughed, "I'll try to have an answer."

"You've done pretty well so far," she observed. "As a matter of fact, it occurs to me you have yet to draw a blank when I ask for help. Are you a preacher? Have you been holding out on me?"

"Not intentionally, Erin. God has a calling on my life, but not of a kind that fits any traditional sense, so I am sort of at a loss how to describe it. Besides, I would rather talk about Christ than me – He's the Savior. I can't save anybody!"

"Yep, that fits," she replied.

"Fits what?" he was curious.

"Fits my quietly wise Sweet Talker. Lots of wisdom, but doesn't make waves and goes unnoticed by the world around him. I think I'm marrying a preacher in the making," she stated.

"Maybe," he allowed, "I would never refuse if the Lord directs me that way, but I can't feature anyone wanting to hear what I have to say. It would get me kicked out of churches!"

"Or crucified, if they still did that kind of thing. Seems to me you are on the same path as Jesus walked!"

"Well, I'm trying to follow His example, so that's nice to hear," he said. "Are you sure, you want to join up with a social outcast like me?"

"If you're headed for fights and confrontations, I wouldn't miss it for the world!"

He burst out laughing.

She chuckled, "Besides, I can be your bodyguard!"

"While I don't doubt for one minute you could handle the job, let's hope I don't need one."

"Still, you know I have your back," she underscored.

"Do I ever," he laughed. "There's no one I'd rather trust. What were you gonna ask me?"

"Why wouldn't Jesus make time to see His mother and brothers when they came to see Him? Was He too much of a big shot to greet his family?"

"Oh! No, that's not it. They didn't come to see Him, they came to *collect* Him," he explained.

"The Pharisees wanted to silence Him because He was making them look bad. He called out hypocrites by His very nature; they hated Him. They had approached Mary (apparently Joseph was dead and gone, since he was out of the picture), saying Jesus had lost His mind, so His family needed to step up and take responsibility for Him. The family was there to haul Him off to the rubber room, so to speak."

"You're kidding! Oh, that's dirty pool!" She was outraged, "Turning His family against Him…that's not right! Why did they believe these Pharisees? Didn't they know Him better than that?"

"I guess not. They knew He was different from them and always had been. Different is often seen as weird; unbalanced is only one step further. It had been thirty years or more since the angel had told Mary how special Jesus would be; there was no telling how much of that encounter she retained, at that point.

"A working-class family keeping their noses to the grindstone might not know what He was doing; anyway, they bought the Pharisees' story, so they attempted to uphold their familial responsibilities. Maybe they listened to His teaching and understood they had been duped, because it seems they left without Him and never tried again. I suspect they had their eyes opened for the first time!"

"Did He and his family ever get on the same page?" she wanted to know.

"Not before His death," he replied. "Mary was one of the first to learn of His resurrection, directly from the mouth of another angel! That must have changed everything for them. All his brothers came to believe in Him afterwards. Two books in the Bible were written by two of His brothers, James and Jude. They weren't part of the twelve, but they lived as believers in Christ, ministering His gospel until they died."

"Wow! Well, that's some comfort. What the Pharisees did crossed a line, in my book," she fumed.

"They only get worse, as you read. Jesus never went easy on them; you could even say He antagonized them. He came to die on the cross for our sins; only folks who hated His guts would do that to Him. What He did causes folks like me to love Him, but what He said causes others to hate Him with a passion! Whatever capacity is in you, He will bring it out for all to see. It's called making all things manifest."

"Hmm. Well, I'll let you rest awhile longer. Thank you for your help; I can't imagine trying to do this without you. Then again, if it weren't for you, I probably wouldn't want to do this at all. See what you put me through?" she laughed.

"It is *so* worth it, Genie," he assured her. "Talk to you soon."

CHAPTER 26

E rin applied herself to the goal she had set with a single-minded determination that had seen her through many grueling matches. She felt like she was being congratulated by Jesus Himself when He told the disciples the reason for His parables, how what others struggled to understand, they were given comprehension.

She had no trouble with the meaning of those things; she recalled Allen's acknowledgment that God was responding to her request, teaching her. It was comforting, even kind of awe-inspiring, but she didn't let the thought distract her from her self-assigned mission.

She was struck by the callousness of Herodias' daughter. She had known many attractive young women who were anything but, when it became apparent what made them tick; but to ask for the execution of a man who meant nothing to her, just to please her vindictive mother? She would have been better off without a mom, like Erin.

She wondered if perhaps she had been spared, not knowing her mom, if she might have been an evil influence like that. She smiled when she thought of Miss Ruth; she had a mom now, as far as she was concerned. It comforted her.

When Jesus confronted the religious hypocrites about making excuses, rather than caring for their aging parents, her heart swelled with pride that Allen did what he could for Ruth. He is an honorable man, she thought; no wonder I love him!

The paradox hit her, how Jesus, although admittedly homeless, used His supernatural power to feed thousands who came to hear Him speak! Surely He could have raised a palace of His own, but He only seemed concerned for His followers. She found Him intriguing.

The repeated mention of demon-possessed people disquieted her. When she reached the account in chapter seventeen of a child being victimized by one who kept trying to burn or drown him, she made a mental note to ask Allen what was up with all this. Jesus seemed to draw these encounters like a magnet, while all the other history she had learned never mentioned such phenomena.

Hollywood made movies to scare people, but movies are just entertainment; you can't believe that nonsense. If what she was reading was true, then demons must be real, too. One thing stood out clearly: Jesus never had any problem getting rid of demons, even when His disciples did. She would get back to this subject.

She was in chapter eighteen when the phone rang.

"Good morning," Allen greeted her, "how's it going?"

She laughed, "Good afternoon, you mean. I think I'm making good time. Your timing is perfect, because I do have a question. Did you rest okay, with my interruptions?"

"I slept well, thank you. Hearing your voice every time I woke up was reassuring. It let me know you're okay, so I was able to drop right off when I lay back down. Maybe I should start calling you every time I wake up!"

"Sounds good to me," she chuckled. "I'm in chapter eighteen. He seems to be repeating stuff He said awhile back. Does He think He didn't make His point well enough before?"

"He sometimes does that to emphasize stuff He considers important. I'm looking it up now to see the context, but if you want to read it to me, it'll catch me up to where you are."

She proceeded to read the chapter to him.

"Haven't you found it yet? I expected you to stop me when you caught up to where I am."

"Why would I do that?" he inquired. "I love the sound of your voice, Erin." She snorted, then giggled as he continued, "You can laugh, but I'm serious. If I can't look into your eyes right now, at least I can soak in the sound of you. I'll take what I can get!"

The mirth stopped, "You're sweet. What you're really saying is you miss me. I miss you, too."

They were silent a moment, then he acknowledged, "You do get me, lady.

"Okay. He was speaking to crowds earlier, telling them how a change of heart must accompany meaningful service to God, or it will be no better than hypocrisy. God can never be fooled!

"This time He is talking to His disciples. They are wondering how to excel in God's sight to receive promotion and become greater than their brethren. If salvation is the gift of God, not one's own doing, how can you wear it better than anyone else? The idea is ludicrous! One who is looking to promote himself is no longer focused on Christ, the Author of salvation, if he ever was at all.

"To be of the same mind as Him, my concern should mirror what matters to Him. So, what matters to Him? People, particularly those in need that can't help themselves. Children epitomize the needy; as our hearts are moved on their behalf, so we should be moved to do what the Lord enables us to do for those lost in sin.

"If we brush them aside, we have a hand in their demise if they miss heaven and will accompany them into hell! They, at least, can say they didn't know what they were doing, but what excuse can we make? They just didn't warrant our attention? Christ died for them, so they warranted His!"

"Oh, wow! 'Who is the greatest?' is the last thing they should have asked Him."

"Yep, but because they did, He was able to make His priorities known to us in scripture, so their mistake served a purpose. Sometimes I wonder if He chose those twelve simply because they would make the right mistakes, so He could manifest His glory! The idea gives me some comfort in my own inadequacies."

"Okay, so He still isn't telling anyone to maim himself, then?"

"No, Genie, He is just underscoring the deadliness of sin. There are sins of commission and sins of omission, but it is all disobedience to the heart of God, separating us from Him. If our body keeps taking us down those paths, it would be better to lose the offending member than be destroyed for doing what comes naturally – that's how vital it is to put away sin!

"But the real solution is to repent and receive Christ, who forgives our sins, covering them with His shed blood at the cross. Once He abides in us, what matters to Him will matter to us!"

"So, lay up treasures in heaven, or go with people that mean nothing to you to hell," she thought aloud. "People are at the center of His thoughts, it seems."

"That's where His concern centers," he affirmed. "You are getting a good picture of where He stands."

"Okay, well, I'm gonna get back to reading. Thanks for calling. It means a lot to know you're in my corner. Talk again soon."

She took a break and made some food before settling down to read. As she completed the chapter, it jarred her how Jesus depicted the importance of forgiving others. You could be forgiven, but if you refused to forgive someone else, your own forgiveness would be revoked! Nothing He said so far came across as plainly as this principle.

What if you had been badly wronged, like her parents abandoning her? That was a dull ache she had never entirely left behind. She wasn't sure she could ever forgive them, even if she wanted to. Did that disqualify her from coming to Christ, if she chose to do so? Well, she would cross that bridge when she came to it; she needed to make an informed decision first.

It amused her when Jesus told the hypocrites that tax collectors and prostitutes would precede them into heaven; she thought, in that case, I might have a chance! It was important to her that she could choose Christ, if she wanted. When one runs out of options, her path is plotted for her; choices are the substance of freedom.

As she read chapter 24, all the ease with which she had sailed through the book dissipated. Future events were described that would begin to make sense, then gave way to doomsday-like warnings to flee without looking back and watch out for deceivers. It was clear Jesus predicted He would return to earth, but even that seemed muddled. He would come flashing across the sky like lightning, yet every eye would see Him and all the tribes of the earth would have time to mourn? That sounded contradictory.

When she asked God to explain this stuff, she found herself dialing Allen without remembering when she picked up her phone. This is weird, she thought, but it's probably what I would have ended up doing anyway.

CHAPTER 27

It was about 8:35 p.m. Allen answered cheerfully, "Hi, Genie! How's it going?"

"Well," she replied, "if God was explaining this to me, I think He took a break. I am totally lost at chapter twenty-four."

"Understandable," he chuckled, "that is all prophecy. It's a study all its own. Some of it is specifically for the Jews and the inhabitants of Jerusalem. If you want, I'll give you an overview to fill in the big picture, but there is a lot you don't need to be concerned with right now. Does that sound good?"

"Please," she implored him, "I'm really trying to finish this. I can see I am close to the end!"

"Can I make a suggestion, Erin?"

"What's that?"

"If God is taking a break, maybe you should, too. Your goal, as I understood it, was to decide whether to receive Christ, not just to finish Matthew. You have taken in a great deal of information today, but that doesn't mean you're any closer to a decision. When we're done talking, why not put the book down for the night and digest what you read?"

She heaved a sigh of relief, "I'll do that, Sweet Talker. I *was* pushing myself to finish Matthew; I kind of forgot that wasn't the point of all this. Thanks for renewing my focus."

"No problem. For the record, I'm really proud of you for what you have undertaken! You will be into the crucifixion account after this, pretty heavy stuff! A night's sleep will help with your perspective."

"Can't argue with that, since it helped you say yes to me."

"It was the second-best decision I ever made. I am so glad you broke tradition to ask me."

She laughed, "Someone had to pop the question. I got impatient. I knew what I wanted, you, and I'm not getting any younger!"

In a cracked, elderly voice he told her, "That's okay, Grandma. I'll comfort you in your old age!"

Whip quick she came back, "Watch it, buddy, you're on thin ice now. I'll always be able to kick your butt!"

He burst out laughing, "Well, if you do, I'm sure it will be because I gave you good reason. Me Foot In Mouth, remember, Warpaint?"

That got both of them laughing.

"Okay. I think the big thing for you to take away from chapter twenty-four is Jesus' return and visitation. His return is when He will remain on earth to rule over it from Jerusalem."

"He plans to do that?" she broke in.

"Yes. Several other passages refer to it. When the tribes of the earth mourn at the sign of the Son of man in the sky, when every eye beholds Him, His return is the event being described. He will set up His kingdom to rule the earth for one thousand years; it is called the millennium reign."

"Well, no one can say He doesn't think big," she observed.

"Oh, there's more," he added. "Before that, at some point, He will visit the earth like a flash of lightning, calling His faithful to meet Him in the air. It will be over before anyone else realizes it is happening. He will take us to heaven instantly; the earth will go through the Great Tribulation in our absence. This is the event commonly referred to as the Rapture."

"Now that seems far-fetched, Allen. You expect to go in this thing? You would leave me behind, if it's real?"

"If you chose to stay, yes, I would," he said honestly. "At His appearing, when He calls, I will only have eyes for Him! I have waited for that moment my whole life; it is my prior commitment that takes precedence over everything else, even you, as much as you mean to me. It's never been a secret, what He means to me. Your study will reveal why He means everything to me. It just matters to me that you know He does!"

"Oh, I believe you," she said. "How will you meet Him in the air, exactly? It doesn't seem possible."

" '*In a moment, in the twinkling of an eye, we shall all be changed and be caught up to the Lord in the air; so shall we ever be with Him.*' It seems impossible, until you think of all the other impossibilities He accomplished. Just in what you read today, think of how He healed people from disabilities, illness, even diseases, like leprosy. Each of those healings was impossible by human standards, yet He did it so often that it was condensed into a single phrase over and over, 'He healed them all!'

"That's not even considering His other miracles. I am convinced, based on His record and promises kept, that if He says He will do something, He'll make it happen."

"How do you know His healings weren't a scam?"

"No one, not even those who hated Him, accused Him of that. If He left any question of faking it, that's not something they would have let pass."

"I guess not," she admitted.

"One more thing I'd like to bring out about this chapter, Erin, is the parable of the fig tree. I don't know if you need it right now, but I want you to know. The fig tree symbolized the nation of Israel in Old Testament prophecy, the land and its borders with its citizenry. In chapter twenty-three, He cursed a fig tree in the presence of His disciples so it died.

"The Pharisees asked for a sign. He told them that as Jonah was in the fish's belly for three days, so He would be in the earth, dead, for three days before rising again. The hypocrites would get no other sign, but the disciples saw Him speak death to the fig tree. He then declared the current generation would see Israel destroyed, for its rejection of Him as the Lamb of God, the long-awaited Messiah.

"Thirty-seven years later, the Roman Emperor Titus laid siege to Jerusalem and destroyed it. The temple was dismantled so completely that not one stone of it was left upon another, as Jesus said it would be. Israel ceased to exist as a nation; it died, just like that fig tree.

"Millions died trying to defend the city, but not one Christian was among them. Believing Jesus' prophecy, they used the intervening years to evacuate; they were gone before the invasion came."

"That's amazing!" she gasped. "How do you know they all got away?"

"The survivors of the siege said so. They had lost everything! It was a sore point that Christians had not stood with them or suffered loss with them."

"Didn't the Christians warn them it was coming?" she checked.

"I'm sure they tried. The warnings would be based on Jesus' prophecy. Having rejected Him, they never did believe what He said."

"How sad!"

"Yes, but despite His accuracy, most people still don't believe His word.

"That's history, then there is the parable in chapter twenty-four. When a fig tree coming out of winter begins to put forth leaves, to show signs of life, you know summer is near. The fig tree symbolizes Israel as a nation, remember? It showed no signs of life until 1948, when it was re-established by U.N. decree. Israel was immediately attacked by its neighbors. Fighting to survive is one of the most distinct signs of life!

"Jesus said the generation this event marked would not pass away until all His words are fulfilled, including His return to set up His kingdom on earth. Are you with me so far?"

She replied, "Yeah, it makes sense, I think. What are you getting at?"

"Just this, Genie, the generation born in 1948 turned 70 years old in 2018. If they are not going to pass away until all Jesus predicted takes place, He is getting down to the wire!"

"You're excited, aren't you, love?" she said.

"Yes, I am, and tickled to share it with you, Erin. I hope we can go in the Rapture together! I want to see Him, but I'd love never to be parted from you, either. If I have treasure in heaven, I hope it's you!"

"You are always so sweet to me," she smiled. "I'm going to think about all I've read and what you've told me. Thank you for helping me, also for the idea of stopping where I am tonight. I can be demanding, especially of myself! You have been a comfort to me today, you know?"

"Thank you," he told her, "that's nice to hear. Sleep well; I'm praying for you, even while you rest."

"Have a nice night!" she said.

She did some stretches and cardio while mulling over what her man told her. He expects to be whisked off without notice into another existence by a Man who hasn't been seen in two thousand years! Absurd, on the face of it, but the dreams she had didn't fit any other explanation. That was provided by the man *in* the dreams, who is now real and to whom she is engaged!

Reality itself had become absurd for her. How do you know what to believe when it's all unbelievable? She had to commit to believe something, if she planned to wed a man straight out of her imagination! A wry grin formed as she considered the odd nature of her conundrum. How on Earth had she come to this point?

She shook her head as sweat soaked her body on the exercise bike she operated. As downright weird as her life had become, she welcomed the changes. How could she not? She wasn't alone anymore. That felt good from the inside out! She chuckled aloud as she thought, "If Allen is a nut, he's *my* nut!"

But if he's unstable, how does talking with him stabilize *me* every time? Perhaps I'm not just more hard-headed than he is, I'm nuttier than he is, too! She laughed at the thought; Allen would get a kick out of that.

As she headed for the shower, she reflected on the day's study. Jesus was intriguing to her for several reasons: His selflessness, His concern for others, His regard for His heavenly Father, and what stood out most to her – His fearlessness. He didn't just buck the religious establishment, He called them out for the *specifics* of their hypocrisy and corruption. He physically attacked their business front in the temple!

Allen said *she* was bold? Jesus took boldness to the next level, living dangerously! Self-preservation should have led to His withdrawal; instead, He warned His followers He was moving toward His death, never turning aside. Allen said He came to die, but it would have taken nerves of steel to walk straight into the hornet's nest without flinching!

She acknowledged she couldn't do it, couldn't imagine a motive compelling enough to try. But *Jesus did it because it was the Father's wish that He be sacrificed for the sins of all mankind*, yet most people would never care!

The Man had heart, for sure, but nothing about it made it personal for Erin. She didn't feel she could make a meaningful commitment to Christ over His ideology. She couldn't really dispute the historical account; it's just that she couldn't quite tie His life to hers. What was the connection? For her, it needed to be personal or it would be phony, and she knew she would renege without that personal connection.

Allen filled her thoughts again. She smiled as she thought what he would say, "Rest, Genie, it'll keep until tomorrow." Yes, it certainly would.

CHAPTER 28

The next morning was Sunday. Many Christians would be attending church, but Allen would respond to her call. He said there was no place for him there; all he would be permitted to do was warm a pew and put money in the offering plate. He missed the worship, but remarked on the irony of being overcome by loneliness while in the midst of a multitude. He would rather seek Christ in solitude without distraction.

She had asked what was special about the Church if it was so impersonal. He told her that the Church of scripture and the church on the corner were not the same. Willing submission to Jesus united His Church, not the walls of a building. All she knew was that no member of any congregation had ever touched her so deeply or made such an impression as Allen and Ruth. She respected their authenticity. She knew she was biased by love, but that had nothing to do with her assessment in this area.

She worked out with weights for strength training, a routine necessary to maintain her lifestyle. Remembering her little contest with Allen, she couldn't help smiling. She *wanted* him to know she was stronger than him. That had driven the point home once and for all. She was kind of a showboat; she had no problem admitting it. This body of hers was the product of much hard work. She was proud of the results!

When he accepted what he learned without excuse, she was proud of him, determined not to let him lose face over it. On the other hand, she could have pointed out that with a little training he had the potential to build arm strength beyond what she could match; after all, she was already at her peak of conditioning. She chose to omit that fact because she *liked* being stronger, enjoyed having that edge! That he didn't begrudge it made her love him all the more!

After cleaning up and eating breakfast, she called him. He offered to stay up and go through the remainder of Matthew with her, but she declined. He had worked last night. He needed some rest, but more than that, this was *her* journey. She needed to see it through alone, come to her own conclusions. He respected that, but reminded her he was only a phone call away. She reassured him that was not something she would forget!

"Now go to bed and get some rest, you big lunk!" she joked. "I might need you later; if I do, you'll want a clear head to answer my questions."

"Not even married yet and she's bossing me around," he grumbled, "Who does she think she is?"

She laughed out loud, "I'm someone who loves you dearly and wants you to take care of yourself. Do you truly resent that?"

"Of course not, but you don't have to be so bossy," he came back, still grumbling.

"Fine!" she said, "Will you *please* get some rest in case I need you later?"

"Certainly, Genie," now his voice was clear as a bell and pleasant, "all you ever had to do was ask." She sighed in frustration. He started laughing, then she joined in before ending the call.

As she settled in to resume her study, she reminded God of what she was doing. She requested that He would pick it up with her, continue to teach her what it meant. The warmth she felt yesterday returned. Crystal clarity accompanied her reading as she took in the parable of the five wise and five foolish virgins. It was obvious to her that He was talking about the Rapture, revealing that half of those who think they are ready to go when He calls will actually ignore Him, missing out when the time comes!

She thought back to what she read yesterday, that one would be taken and the other left of those who appeared to be together. It reinforced what she was reading now. The thought chilled her! What a devastating thing to be mistaken about. To see Allen disappear, to know he was gone and she was left alone... She couldn't bear to think of it! She read on quickly, trying to put the idea behind her.

His judgment of the nations left no doubt that He did indeed expect to rule the whole world! But His judgment remained in character. How we treat others forms the basis for His verdict, and He takes our actions *personally*. There's that accountability God is known for, where people are held responsible for their actions or recognized for kindnesses shown.

Only the ruler of the world could do these things, and only God would know what people have done in their lives to call them on it; so, Jesus is identifying Himself as both! If He is declaring His future, what is left but to get the present out of the way?

That is just what Matthew did. Erin understood what she read without difficulty. How Judas must have been rattled when he faced Jesus at the Last Supper, only to learn that his betrayal was known!

Jesus' fearlessness, when He knew what was ahead for Him, humbled her even more; but at least His prayers in the garden made it clear how anxious He felt. He was still human, after all, just determined to see it through.

The Jewish kangaroo court in which He was tried made her blood boil. Erin was quick to anger when she saw injustice done!

The Roman governor, Pilate, saw how Jesus was being railroaded, but let it proceed, rather than risk a riot. Pathetically weak, she thought. The Romans were ruthlessly efficient at putting down riots and insurrections. That part of their history was well known, aside from the Bible. Maybe he couldn't have stopped Jesus' execution, since God had decreed it must happen, but he could have shown the gumption to try.

She read how the chief priests mocked him when He was up on the cross, "He saved others, but He cannot save Himself." Didn't they get how they incriminated themselves? He saved others, they admitted, yet they killed Him. How is that right?

Her frustration mounted as she read, until she came to the angel's declaration at the empty tomb. The story had absorbed her to the point that she forgot how it ended. He arose, and that made things right again. The tale was not complete without that detail.

Closing the book, she pondered. She was inclined to believe what she had perused. So many people disparaged the Bible for literally thousands of years, yet no one had ever disproved it once and for all. It wasn't for lack of trying! It had outlasted all its critics. She hadn't seen anything so far that didn't ring true. But somehow, it just didn't seem to apply to her.

She needed something that would tie it to her, something personal that would make calling on Christ more than a ritualistic observance done on the basis of some arcane command. She needed something in all these words she could identify with to move her. She felt like she wasn't finished; moreover, that warm feeling of an unseen presence had not departed! It was time to call Allen, she decided.

When she had him on the phone, she explained everything going on inside her the best she could. It struck her how she had come to trust this man she loved. In times past, she wouldn't have aired her deep uncertainties to anyone, for fear it would make her appear weak. She knew he would not judge her or turn against her. He was a safe zone; he would guard her heart as carefully as she would.

She asked if he had some idea where she could keep reading until she was ready to make a decision. He said he didn't, but offered to pray for some direction. She accepted his offer, then listened as he inquired of God very simply, then went quiet a moment.

"Erin, He's not giving me anything. I don't think He's going to; this is between you and Him. He is leading you! He will drop something into your heart, something you will feel you have to check out. What thoughts are comforting you in your quest for truth?"

She laughed, "*You*, Sweet Talker. The thought of you, the sound of you, how much you mean to me motivates me to keep going until I'm sure what I believe and ready to take a stand! Well, the thought of Mom comforts me, too. Miss Ruth is the kind of Mom I wish I had growing up – wait. Isn't she named after someone in scripture?"

"Yes, she is. Ruth was King David's great-grandmother. There is a tiny little book telling her story in the Old Testament, eight books in, by the same name. It should make a very quick read, if you're interested."

"I am! Let me call you back," she was excited. She felt this was worth a look.

Allen cheered her on, "Good hunting!"

Erin breezed through the four chapters of Ruth. It was like a bed-time story, very easy reading. It touched her, particularly Ruth's devotion to her mother-in-law, so like the bond she felt with Mom. As she slowly reread Ruth's declaration to Naomi, her thought turned to Allen. Something clicked inside her. The vault door of her heart opened and tears ran down her face. She had her personal connection to God, indirect but very real! At last, she was ready to make a commitment she could stand by until the day she died.

Her hands shook as she dialed Allen again. When he answered, she announced, "I found what I needed! Are you ready for this?"

"What have you got, Genie?" he asked.

Her voice quavered as she told him, "Wherever you go, I will go; and wherever you lodge, I will lodge. Your family shall be my family, and your God shall be my God!" He recognized her source material, but she had modified it to make it a personal oath.

He was floored! After a moment he responded, "You mean that, don't you?"

"Yes, I do. Show me what to do, so I can stand with you before Him, and I'll do it." She was basing her faith on her trust in him! It humbled him beyond words.

He told her, "Erin, you honor me so much. I will present *us* to the Lord in prayer, but some of it will have to come from your mouth."

"I understand, husband. I will repeat whatever you say I need to. Don't worry, I won't say anything I don't mean. I trust *you* in this, Sweet Talker!"

He wasn't certain how much weight this carried with the Lord, but he thought that if he guided her hand into His, Jesus would make up whatever was lacking!

He began to pray, "Heavenly Father, Erin and I together present ourselves to you in answer to your call. You have bound us to one another with an unbreakable cord of love. This is Your doing and Yours alone, for which we are both in awe and eternally grateful. Jesus' work at the cross provides us hope we never deserved, but this act of kindness far exceeds any obligation or promise You ever made to us. Thank you, from both of us!"

Erin echoed her thanks.

"This woman You have joined to me has become my greatest earthly treasure, Lord. I offer her to You with her willing agreement; she is far too precious to keep for myself! Please hear her as she offers herself to You."

He asked Erin, "Are you ready, Genie?"

She sniffed; he knew she was crying, "Take it slow so I can keep up, okay?"

"You got it," he replied. This is what they prayed:

"Lord Jesus, I have heard Your gospel. I know I am a sinner, that my sins separate me from You and condemn me to death; but instead, You died in my place. Forgive me for my sins. Cover me with Your righteousness, I pray, that I might live with You forever as Your handmaid, Your warrior…Your daughter." She added "If You will have me."

Shaken by her humble sincerity, he finished, "In Your own holy name, amen." He began to praise and worship Him, comforted by His Spirit. Erin, however, had an entirely separate experience.

CHAPTER 29

F or her, it was as though she entered into a waking dream. She knelt before a figure she couldn't see clearly, because He radiated bright light that pulsed as though alive! She was utterly ashamed, aware that she was naked and filthy, as though she had been wrestling pigs in the mud. The light from the Man before her pulsed bright, enveloping her. When it withdrew, she was spotlessly clean!

A white linen robe was extended toward her. It seemed to absorb some of the light He exuded and glowed on its own. Hands just out of her line of sight helped her stand, then draped the glowing white robe over her.

The Figure spoke, "I have cleansed you of sin. This is My righteousness that covers you now, giving you access to My throne and the throne of My Father."

She was overwhelmed. She tried to speak; it came out as a whisper, "How did I get here?"

She more felt than saw the figure smile, "It wasn't easy, but you came through the strait gate. I have opened your eyes to see how constrained your entry was; this was the *only* way you would have heeded My call."

She comprehended what He was saying and gasped; her acceptance of grace had never hung by more than a thread!

He laughed, a sound of pure joy that embedded itself in her soul. "Be at peace. That which made you so hesitant to call My name and limited your chance for salvation also serves to make you fiercely loyal. You are Mine now by your own choice, a choice you will never renege on!"

He used the word she had thought when considering her decision about Him. He knew what she had feared; moreover, He banished that fear with His statement.

He pinned her down now with her words, "Did you mean what you said to Me?"

"Yes, Lord."

"You will be My handmaid?"

"Yes, Lord!" She saw an image of Allen beside Christ. He was in pain, his arms wrapped around his torso, as if he had suffered a wound and was struggling to keep upright. Her heart broke at the sight.

The Lord told her, "Then comfort My wounded servant. You and I will bind up his broken heart, together."

"Oh, yes, Lord, gladly!" He nodded.

"You will be My warrior?"

"If I can, Lord." She wasn't sure what that meant.

He seemed to pull a sword out of His mouth, then handed it to her. "This is My weapon of choice," He assured her.

She felt clumsy as she tried to swing it around.

He chuckled, "No, child. Just aim it at whatever threatens and hold on to it tightly! It will obtain victory every time on its own, as long as you don't let go of it!"

She looked down toward it in wonder, but this time there was no sword. Her Bible was in her hands!

His hand reached out to brush her face tenderly. "You *are* My daughter, Erin. You always have been! Welcome home!"

CHAPTER 30

Tears obscured her vision as the assurance was driven deep into her heart that she was once and for all *accepted*. She blinked the tears away to find herself back at home with the phone to her ear. Allen was giving praise to God. Erin joined in, overflowing with gratitude. For the first time, the two of them worshiped God together, adding another level to the bond they shared.

When it ended, she asked emphatically, "Why didn't you tell me God was like this?"

He was caught totally off guard; all that came out of his mouth was "Uh-"

She started laughing gleefully. He realized he'd been had, which got him laughing with her.

"You're gonna have me rejoicing over you the rest of my life now, you know that?"

"Good! You could use some joy in your life! You know what? This time you didn't just overcome, you won! You won me, for yourself and Christ both! How does it feel to be a winner?"

He couldn't stop laughing. He finally managed one word, "Fantastic!" Pure joy expressed itself as laughter at both ends of the connection, until they recovered enough to reaffirm the love they shared.

She laid out everything she had experienced in the Lord's presence. He was in awe! He told her that most folks have a moment with Him at salvation, but He had revealed Himself to her in an extremely personal way.

She said, "I needed that, Allen! He showed me that I never would have come to Him, if He hadn't put such a love for you in me, then led me to Ruth's example of devotion. A single thread of occurrences was the only way I would accept salvation, so He guided my life along that thread until I knelt in His presence. I'm fifty-four years old, but He has been planning my homecoming all my life!

"I realize your divorce caused you pain, and I'm sorry. But if He hadn't brought us together, I was hopeless, bound for hell! He has been in control of your life, even when it seemed to go sour, my love. You were the one witness to His grace I would listen to, so He made room in your life for me. You are an amazing man! You gave me your heart without holding back in the slightest!"

She chuckled, "I never had a chance of resisting you, either, Sweet Talker! What do you think of that?"

He had no words. He sniffled as she continued, "Your broken heart is in our hands, love. He's gonna let me help put it back together. Prepare to be loved like you have never been loved before, boy! Spiritually, physically, in every way one person can love another, you're gonna get it from me! Covering your face with kisses was only the mildest taste of the affection and care I will show you in the life we share together! No man of mine is going to end his days with a broken heart, you get me?"

He cracked up laughing again, "I've been threatened with worse; I suppose I'll survive!"

"Yes, you will," she came back. "Sadness is not going to be a way of life for you anymore, my man. I won't allow it! As Christ's handmaid, I've been assigned to comfort you. You better believe I take that assignment seriously!"

"Then the job will get done, I have no doubt," he predicted. "Christ never sends His servants on a task without equipping them to accomplish it. Judging from the amount of joy you've already provided me, I know I'm going to be one happy fellow! I love you, Erin, more than words can ever express."

"No, words aren't gonna cover it," she agreed, "guess we're just gonna have to get married. Let's do that!"

"But I'm already engaged! What should I tell her?"

"Marry her, you dope! You can see me on the side!"

"You two will wear me out," he objected.

"Oh, that's a given, sweetheart," she told him, "but what a way to live! You'll never wonder if you're wanted, and I won't tell her if you don't!"

Dropping the game, he confessed, "I'm glad there's only one of you. I think I'm gonna have my hands full!"

"Don't flatter yourself, love. I'm way more than you can handle! I'll be doing the handling. You will be hanging on for dear life, and you'll love every minute of it!"

"I'm not sure if there's a dignified way to respond to that, Erin, so I'll just say thank you in advance and shut my mouth before I embarrass myself."

She gave a little laugh, "I am marrying a wise man! I'll never rob you of your dignity... in public."

"Wait one minute! Don't I get some respect in private, too?"

She snickered, "Tell you what; I'll respect you in the morning!"

"And handle me at night," he filled in.

"Uh-huh," she agreed.

"I think that's the best I'm gonna get. Can we change the subject now?"

She burst out laughing, "Had enough of my teasing, have you?"

"For the moment, I am as uncomfortable as I care to be. It'll be more fun after the wedding, when you can finish what you start!"

"Yeah, it will," she said. "Of course, if you want to move the date up, I'm open to discussion."

"Erin, I wouldn't mind setting an earlier date, if you like, and Christ is good with it; but not because I'm so aroused I can't wait!"

"Then I'll ease up, Sweet Talker. I didn't mean to bug you that much!"

"Thank you," he replied, relieved to hear her concession. "Dear Lord, if you can wind me up so much just talking to me, what am I in for when you're touching me, too?"

"Don't worry about it," she advised. "No matter how hard it is to take, at that point I'll make sure you don't have to endure it for long."

"Now that's comforting to hear," he admitted. "I'm beginning to understand why you warned me to be careful what I wish for, Genie. Sometimes you're a little scary."

"I can come on really strong; I know that. But Allen, you have nothing to fear from me. No matter how intimidating you find my capabilities, I'll always be your Genie; the woman who loves you with every fiber of her being! You have given me your trust, more precious to me than gold. I am determined to be worthy of it!

"If something I do is too much for you, I will adjust whatever I need to, in order to accommodate you; that's how important you are! If you're ever truly afraid of me, then I have failed to provide you the security you deserve as my partner, the one who stands at my side! It would break my heart to fail you that way; besides, I never want to have to try to explain that kind of failure to the Lord Jesus I just met! I don't think my tears would ever stop!"

"Wife, honor your husband as the weaker vessel," he rephrased the scriptural command.

"Exactly! That's what I'm saying, and trying to do, because you're worth it. I value you that much! I don't ever want to give you cause to flinch from me, even when you are deliberately annoying! I can put you in your place playfully. There is no need or desire in me to hurt you, my sweet man. Please don't ever be afraid to tell me if I scare you. I promise, I can and want to be better than that!"

"That was the first scripture we ever discussed, remember?" he said.

"I do," she replied.

"From the time I explained its meaning, you took it to heart," he noted, "even though you had no obligation to do so, since you didn't believe in Christ then. You knew you were stronger than me, so you voluntarily submitted to its instruction. You have honored me ever since."

"I wanted to," she confirmed. "It seemed so beautiful and right to me, and I knew you believed in the Bible it came from. It pleased me to respect your belief, although I admit I got a kick out of turning it around on you to point out that I'm the stronger partner!

"I am proud of my strength and my man-defeating skills, Allen, though that seems petty now. That hasn't changed in me, either, even if I don't lord it over you. It's just that you are mine, so I have exempted you from receiving the kind of punishment I can dish out!"

"Well, *there* is a definite advantage to being your favorite guy," he observed.

She chuckled.

"Like I said before, I'm proud of your strength, too, even if it causes me to feel a bit inadequate. You worked very hard to hone yourself into the weapon you are today. You should be proud! As long as pride doesn't exalt itself against God or express itself in mistreating others, there is nothing wrong with it. Pride is what motivates a craftsman to turn out exceptional work. From what you have told me, your company sets a standard for integrity, mistreating customers only as they wish!"

She started laughing, "I never heard it described that way!"

"I don't think I'll ever understand your clientele. You think maybe they are a bit brain damaged before you ladies rough them up?"

"It's possible, but their money is green, so we're happy to take it! As far as my causing you to feel inadequate, let me explain something. I never wanted my physical match for a life partner! I *like* being stronger – all I ever wanted was for my man to be okay with that!

"Allen, nothing about you has been a disappointment to me, so far. There is no good reason for you to feel inadequate. We may not be a stereotypical couple, but we're happy, aren't we? If God brought us together, surely He knew what He was doing! You are so good for me; try to remember that, okay?"

"I'll try," he said. "You aren't going to let me forget it, anyhow."

"No, I'm not," she smiled. "You helped me come to Christ, made me your treasure for eternity. I will treasure you as long as we live. Don't beat yourself up! I'm much better equipped to do it than you are! If I'm not doing it, take the hint – you must not deserve that kind of treatment!"

He laughed, "Now there's some logic I never considered before! If she doesn't beat me up, I must be doing something right. What happens when I do something wrong, make you angry? It's inevitable, you know. Every couple fights, occasionally."

"Would you ever hit me?" she asked.

"Of course not!" He responded instantly. "I don't hit women; it's wrong! I was raised not to hit anyone, but especially not girls; and you never, ever hit your wife! Do you think I would ever hit you? Have I –"

"Time out!" she pleaded, "I know you wouldn't. See, some things are set in your mind ahead of time. I'm the same way. You are bound to anger me sooner or later, but violence is not on the table as an option for me, either. You are always safe with me, lover, even when I'm not in the mood to kiss you. I'm bound to make you angry sometimes, too. You're not the only one who can control his temper!"

"Touché," he said. "I guess we're still getting to know each other. I must seem awfully insecure to you."

"No, I don't think so," she said thoughtfully. "What we have together is so extraordinary, I think we both see it as too good to be true. We keep expecting something to go wrong. You're afraid of being hurt again, emotionally, I mean; and I'm afraid – I'm not sure what I'm afraid of! Maybe I'm afraid I'm going to suddenly wake up to discover this was all just another dream! That would be such a letdown!"

"Erin, look at your ring," he directed. "I have one that matches yours. This is real, just like my adoration for you, just like I am. You just knelt before Christ Himself, who you didn't even believe in before today. He never appeared in your dreams, He just inserted me into them, remember? It's all real. August is coming. Soon you'll be an old married woman who can only get out of the bed on one side without climbing over me!"

She cracked up laughing as he continued, "You'll have to share the bathtub and lavatory, taking turns with me on the toilet. When we go out, you'll have the option of getting in on the passenger side, if you like. Instead of being hit on by strangers, you'll just have me hugging and kissing you spontaneously, holding your hand and putting my arm around you companionably.

"Your decisions will have to be spoken aloud, if you want me to know what you're doing; you will likewise expect me to clue you in on mine. You'll get help with chores, but much less alone time, especially with Ruth around. There will be conversations, foot rubs, massages and cuddling that will take getting used to, along with a pesky husband that seems to follow you around and keeps trying to take your clothes off!"

She had been giggling, but that got her laughing hard. "Oh, you laugh now, but it can be a real pain when you are dressed for the day, then he starts messing with your ensemble. That's reality, girl, not just another dream you can escape by simply waking up! You sure this is what you want?"

Still laughing, she told him, "Are you kidding? You just described heaven on earth to me, Sweet Talker! I can hardly wait for August to get here!" They talked a few minutes more before saying goodbye.

CHAPTER 31

When Erin sat down to write the news of her engagement this time, it was ridiculously easy. Not only did it practically write itself, revisiting her journey to the present gave her a fresh appreciation for what Christ had put together on her behalf. It read like a fairy tale; all she had done was walk a path laid out for her by the supernatural Father who welcomed her with open arms!

As she proofread it, she was struck by the joy that permeated its content. What she felt in her heart came through in her announcement. The overtone was unlike anything she had ever written. She recognized that something inside her was fundamentally changed. Her life had a heartfelt direction, a sense of completeness that had never been there before!

She posted it with satisfaction. Since it was written from her perceptions, not Allen's, any mockery that came of it would target her. That suited her just fine, since she wanted him spared. Any who dared to disparage her were welcome to *bring it*; she would quickly put them in their place! She built this little world of hers and had earned its respect – there was no way she would tolerate anything less!

In the days afterward, she noticed other changes, primarily her own perspective. She still loved the physicality of her sport, the exertion and competition; but humiliating the guys she defeated made her uncomfortable. She didn't personally take on many opponents nowadays, but some requested her specifically on a regular basis. Their loyalty stemmed from long acquaintance with her personally.

It was funny, in a way; friendships had come into being with customers who liked her, respecting her ability to *flatten them and make them suffer!* They appreciated her for the treatment they received, coming back for more; some declared their love for her! She was fond of them for getting attached to her – who doesn't like loyal customers?

Maybe Allen had a point, these guys came in with pre-existing brain damage! In that case, she was providing a kind of care for them, she reflected. There were women out there who would not only humble them for a session, they would do them lasting harm. Her girls were never going to rob or blackmail guys that came in trusting them to be honorable in their conduct. Some crazy things took place in this industry; some of the more ruthless athletes out there were no better than seductive muggers!

Her taunts became less personal and insulting, instead focusing on the situations her clients found themselves in and their inability to break free. Some commented on her attitude change with appreciation; one said that in losing (as usual, he laughed), it was nice to walk away feeling like he wasn't that bad, she was just that *good*! It was satisfying to hear him say that, to know she didn't cause him shame.

She had never been as verbally abusive in her beatdowns as some other wrestlers, but now she saw how tasteless verbal abuse was, so she deliberately avoided it. When overhearing it in other girls' matches, now it just seemed nasty; but she had trained them. They learned that from her, too, so they wouldn't understand attempts to dial back their intensity.

More had changed for her, as well. Cursing grated on her nerves. She used to laugh when others did it; truthfully, she could peel the paint off walls when the mood hit her! It seemed stupid and pointless, now, very unprofessional – even childish! There was no sense trying to clean it up, because the customers themselves brought it in and would disrespect her girls if they didn't respond in kind.

The girls could eventually be brought on board a campaign to clean up the language, would enjoy penalizing guys for cursing with additional pain; but that kind of campaign would require a commitment from her that she wasn't willing to make. She was on her way out to make a life with Allen. It wasn't the time to make alterations in a business she was leaving to others.

Besides, such a change might well run off some customers. When these guys are getting hurt, they vent. Demanding they watch their language doesn't make sense!

It was time to walk away, she decided. She had outgrown this phase of her life. She was ready to move on, yearned to be away in the arms of the man she loved. Stefanie had day to day operations well in hand, only needing Erin's help in booking special events. Erin's name and reputation opened doors that weren't available to Stef, but her cell phone could reach out from Missouri just as easily as it could from L.A.

She discussed her thoughts with Allen, asking if the guest room was still available for an extended stay. He was delighted, said it was ready whenever she was. She requested that he not tell Ruth, yet. She wanted to talk to her, to make sure she was still welcome. Allen snorted, said of course she was, but agreed to Erin's request.

Due to appointments, engagements and extensive arrangements with her attorney and accountant, it would be three weeks from the time she left Springfield to her reunion with Allen and Ruth. If it was going to be the three of them facing life together, she had a *lot* to bring to the table to make them all comfortable; getting it organized required planning at this end.

When she called Ruth, she had a hard time holding her composure. The elder woman got excited when Erin asked if she could come to stay, told her that was a silly question! Ruth said she had missed her, was anticipating having another girl to visit with in the house. Erin promised she would not be a burden, but was told she was talking foolishness again, so just stop!

They talked a good while after that, which caused Erin to remember how this woman had come to mean so much to her. She was homesick by the time the call ended; she knew she had made the right decision. It was time to go to her new home!

She flew this time. When Allen picked her up at the airport, he acted as though it was years since he held her in his arms, rather than weeks. He held her a long time. The picture of him standing as though wounded next to Christ came back to mind. She understood then how he needed her, so she held him patiently, giving him the comfort of her embrace.

When it became awkward, she looked him in the eye, "If you don't leggo my eggo, I'm gonna kiss your whole face!"

He looked a bit shocked, then grinned, stepping back quickly, "You would, too, wouldn't you?"

She chuckled, "Try me!"

"Not here, thank you very much!"

Gathering her baggage, they loaded it in the van. On the way home, she informed him that they needed to discuss some important matters concerning the days ahead; nothing earthshaking, she reassured him, just how she would fit in to the household as a family member, instead of a guest.

He said okay, then stated that Ruth had something she wanted to talk to the two of them about when they got home. She had clammed up when he wanted to know more, saying it was for both of them.

Upon arrival, Erin received a warm greeting and a big hug from Ruth. Allen had set up a vanity in the spare room for her use. When he apologized for not decorating more, she thanked him for his thoughtfulness with a hug and kiss. There was an oversized dresser for her clothes. She told him they would take care of the blank walls together. Once her luggage was in, Ruth was waiting for them in the living room.

They settled on the couch, holding hands as she spoke, "Kids, Mom's going to be a busybody for a change. I know you are old enough to make your own decisions. I respect that, but none of us are getting any younger. I believe Christ will be calling us home soon; son, I know you believe it, too."

He nodded while Erin watched him, wide-eyed. She was still getting used to the idea of the Rapture. They had studied scripture together, ever since her salvation. She knew she would be included in His call, so she soaked up every bit of information she could about it.

Ruth went on, "My point is, if you two are living under the same roof, why don't you go ahead and get married now? I know nothing shameful is happening between you, but in my opinion, it serves no purpose to keep each other waiting for months. If I wasn't certain that you are meant for one another, I wouldn't suggest it; but since the hand of God brought you together, why wait any longer?"

Allen looked at Erin. She was grinning from ear to ear and nodded eagerly. "Genie, you had plans for a big wedding," he started.

Squeezing his hand firmly, she said, "I know, but I don't care, love. All that really matters to me is that we're together. Let's not put it off! The way you held me at the airport is the way it should always be between us, no distance separating us ever again. Let's make it happen, okay?"

"I'm the last one who needs persuading! I can barely keep my hands off you!"

She laughed as he turned to Ruth, "Will you pray with us about this, Mom? I'm not sure if either of us can be objective enough to make this decision without our desire getting in the way. I think we wanted this all along!"

Erin nodded with a half-smile, "I did, for sure."

Ruth prayed with them. Such peace settled over the room that they began to worship God. When it was done, they were taken with simple joy and found themselves laughing.

She stated the obvious, "I think you have your answer. August gave you a response to Erin's proposal and an opportunity for her to show respect for you when she didn't share your values, but the Lord isn't requiring you to wait."

Erin turned him to face her gently, "You were worth waiting for, Allen. You still are, but let's not, okay?"

"Okay, Mrs. Edwards. I don't think I have it in me to ever say no to you."

CHAPTER 32

Than was on the Friday she arrived. They married two days later on Sunday. A minister friend of his in Branson conducted the wedding in the afternoon. His youngest brother and his wife attended; there wasn't time for other family members to respond, since they practically eloped! Anthony was his best man. Ruth agreed to be Erin's matron of honor, but when Stefanie flew in and surprised them, she insisted on abdicating her place. She confided to Erin she was concerned she couldn't be counted on, due to her health.

It was the simplest of ceremonies with traditional vows, but they were heartfelt. Everyone was moved by the presence of the Holy Spirit. Allen's sister-in-law commented that royal weddings she had watched on TV did not compare to the raw beauty of this one; Stefanie tearfully agreed. The family had promised to check in on Ruth while they spent two nights in Branson.

Erin had picked out a suit for Allen. She wore a lacy white dress with the grace of a model. Her blonde hair naturally covered her head more beautifully than any artificial covering ever could; she topped it with a wreath of flowers. Utterly breathtaking, she beamed, the joy on her face plain for all to see!

Once they were away to themselves, he asked Erin if she had any regrets about the simplicity of her wedding. Laughing, she kissed him, "Are you kidding, Mr. Edwards? Tens of thousands of dollars and months' worth of planning couldn't have made our wedding more memorable! God was in attendance, in all His glory! Who could ask for more?"

He responded, "I just want you to be happy, Mrs. Edwards, as happy as you have made me!"

"I'll *show* you how happy I am. Call me Genie and take me to our room. I'm gonna grant you some wishes!"

That's when he discovered just how magical she could be, and how easily she could render him speechless!

When they were lying in each other's arms afterward, she asked him, "So what do you want to do now, with your life, I mean?"

He grinned up at her, "You say that like you think I might survive the way you're assaulting me!"

She cracked up laughing, then covered his face with kisses while he squirmed to no avail. When she stopped, she assured him, "Oh, you'll live through it, I promise. God wouldn't have brought us together if I was bad for your heart; besides, I know CPR!"

"You're telling me there's no escape, then," he smiled.

"None! I have you now; I'm not about to let you go. Even if I gave you the chance to run away, you wouldn't take it. Like you said, I have you hook, line and sinker; what can you do?"

He kissed her and nuzzled her neck, burrowing into her embrace. "You got me. I'll just have to trust you," he told her, looking up into her eyes. With a wide grin, she took his throat in her jaws playfully, then kissed it, working around his neck to his ear. She giggled as he shuddered involuntarily, ending with a hard kiss on the mouth.

"I have so looked forward to having you like this," she told him.

"You're a predator!"

"Uh-huh, and you are my prey. But I'm never going in for the kill – I'm just going to keep devouring you alive!

"But seriously," she rolled off beside him, one arm and one leg still draped across his body, "what do you want to do? We haven't discussed money, but there's something you should know. I have enough for both of us. I wouldn't retire if it was a concern. When we go home, I intend to open a joint account with you at whatever bank you recommend. I made arrangements to establish the account with an EFT of $120, 000."

His jaw dropped; she grinned at his look of shock. "I told you money was not a problem for me; now it isn't for you, either, my love! Much of my worth is tied up in the company, but I figure we can live comfortably on this. $10,000 will be deposited for us monthly to maintain the account against whatever we use."

"My Lord!" he burst out, "You're rich?"

"Yeah, I guess I am," she announced, smiling broadly. "My net worth is $4.7 million. Most is invested, but that produces dividends from which our monthly deposits originate. Taxes will be paid from outside our cost of living account. Do you think $120,000 yearly will support us?"

"Erin, that's four times what I gross annually! It makes my job unnecessary!"

She kissed him again, "I know. That's my point. You don't have to work. I am retiring and I'd like to spend my time with you. Work will take you away from me; I'd rather it didn't. It's your call, Sweet Talker. You provide a worthy service to people in need, which I respect. If you want to continue doing it, I support your choice. At the risk of sounding selfish – I suppose I'm being selfish – I hope you'll quit to be with me!"

"Genie, I had no idea you could do this!"

She chuckled, "I told you I was pretty sure I could blow your mind. I won't lie, I'm having a blast doing it!"

"I can see that," he observed. "Ever since we got in this bed, you just keep doing it!"

She laughed, "I'm not done yet, my sweet man. I'll have you speechless again before I let you up! But I'd like an answer to my question first. Will you retire with me?"

"Erin, the job was just a way to pay the bills. I'm not attached to it. If you want to pay our way and can afford to, and if you don't think less of me in doing so, I'll give my notice. I'm not sure what we'll do with so much time, though. I hope I don't get on your nerves, always being so close. You gotta let me know when you need alone time, and I'll leave the room, okay?"

She nodded, "That's incredibly perceptive for a guy. Same goes for you, understand? I don't want you getting tired of me or feeling smothered."

"I don't think there's much risk of that," he told her.

"Good! I can't feature ever tiring of having you near, either. As for what we'll do, I'm not worried about it. We'll find common ground. Sometimes we'll each do our own thing while just enjoying having the other one near. If God has called you to ministry, maybe bringing us together has taken us a step closer to seeing how it plays out. He brought me home to Him; if He could do that, nothing is too difficult for Him!"

"Your insight is *unbelievable*, Genie. He showed me, over thirty years ago, that all it would take to put me into ministry was one miracle. I replied that was beyond me. He said He knew that, but it's nothing extraordinary for Him; He would do it, when the time comes. I've been waiting on Him ever since!

"A passage in Isaiah promises that whoever waits on Him shall renew his strength, mount up on wings as eagles, run without growing weary and walk without fainting."

Her eyes seemed to glow as she listened.

"Our union has doubled whatever strength I could manage alone, and He promises to renew it before it runs out."

"Our union has *more* than doubled your strength, dear," she corrected him with a sly smile. "I'm stronger than you, remember?"

He shook his head, "I'll never forget that. You take way too much pleasure in reminding me!"

She cracked up laughing, "Yeah, I do."

She began to flex her leg on him. He caught his breath as she watched his face to measure what effect it had. He tried to move it off of him, but it wouldn't budge. Her hand began to explore as he watched her.

She smiled and winked as she continued, "I *do* take pleasure at your expense, don't I? Let me give you some helpful advice, Sweet Talker."

His heart beat faster as she raised up, then leaned over him. With a wolfish grin, her face an inch above his, she whispered, "Get used to it!"

It might be sound advice; he's never quite been able to follow it. She handles him with such ease that it shakes him up every time they make love, but she never hurts him. Her embrace provides a comfort he can't explain afterward.

It never fails to turn out like she promised it would, either. When they leave the bedroom, he knows beyond any shadow of doubt how much he is loved and wanted, even though he's not in control. Not only is he good with that, he finds it exciting. She has his trust; every time she proves herself worthy of it, she affirms the wisdom of his choice!

When God provides that special someone whose loving arms draw you close, whatever rejection you previously experienced becomes irrelevant. He is spirit, yet He is fully aware of our need to be physically held and comforted. He never fails to provide what we need, if we are willing to wait on Him.

So, even though sex has become a bit like getting trounced, he relishes her affection! Even in her forcefulness, she still listens to his voice. Sometimes she invites him to make a wish, allowing him a moment's respite to do so, but when he thinks he might get the upper hand, it always turns out he has played right into hers again! She toys with him and drives him crazy, but her delight in doing so is infectious. He couldn't resent it if he tried!

Her good-natured playfulness set him at ease enough to share what he thought the Lord showed him when she was driving back to California.

CHAPTER 33

After dinner he brought it up, "Do you remember that time I woke up after hearing your voice, back when you were headed home?"

"Oh, yeah! That was weird! You said you thought God was showing you something about me. I was intent on hearing about it when we got back together, but then we decided to get married right away and I forgot. Please, tell me about it!"

"First, I want to thank you for not twisting my arm," he teased.

She gave him a wry smile, "I think you know I was just giving you a hard time."

"I know," he admitted, "but I wouldn't want to put it to the test by dropping the subject now."

She nodded energetically, "Yep, my husband is definitely a wise man. A wise man knows not to provoke his wife. Spill it, buddy!"

He smiled, "Yes, ma'am! I've heard it said on the radio that a man should study his wife to learn what's important to her."

She nodded thoughtfully.

"As I said before, your being physically stronger than me is strange territory; I have no experience to fall back on. I don't resent it..."

"I know that," she said.

"...but I'm not sure how to respond to it. I feel respect and admiration for what you have accomplished."

She smiled, obviously pleased.

"As your husband, I want to be supportive, but I'm not sure how to be. 'Your strength and your skills are what make you exceptional,'; you later expressed that it did portray how you feel. I told you why I don't agree with that statement, but it *matters* to me how you feel."

Her hands reached for his, "I really appreciate that. Thank you, my love!"

"*You* matter to me, sweet lady. If He did show me something, if I got it right – I'm still not sure – I need... no, I *want* to be here for you in every way that's important to you."

She was looking at him curiously now. He was acutely aware how he was stumbling over his words. He felt stupid and his face flushed with embarrassment, but he was determined to see it through.

"I feel so dumb for asking this. I know I'm no challenge for you, but if you are retiring to be with me, leaving behind your lifestyle of choice, would it matter if I'm willing to wrestle with you?"

A look of wonder spread across her face. In a very small voice she asked, "You would do that for me?"

That look was what he needed to see, the reason he didn't tell her on the phone what he was thinking. Now he knew he had truly heard from God!

"Erin, there is nothing I wouldn't do for you, even if it means I will have to endure pain and lose every match I have with you. Please don't hurt me too much, okay?"

She started laughing as tears made their way down her cheeks, "I love you *so much*!" she declared. "You didn't know I wanted this, did you? You really are God's gift to me!"

"I am *so* gonna die," he muttered.

She heard him, squeezed his hands, "Trust me, I know my stuff better than that.

"Let me explain a few things, love. First, I have nothing to prove to you. You *know* I'm stronger and have correctly assumed that my lifetime of practice gives me a huge advantage over you. Second, you are not a paying customer that I am obliged to make sure gets what he paid for, a beatdown to remember!

"For the two of us, this is nothing more than fun exercise and playful competition. I was worried I would lose my edge without practice – it means the world to me that you are willing to be my sparring partner!

"There will be some 'ouch' moments, especially when I'm locking in submission holds, but you will control how much pain you endure. It won't be much at all, unless you're too stubborn to tap out or give up. I will advise you to tap when I have you locked into a hold before I apply pressure – if you take my advice, you'll avoid pain!"

"That's comforting to hear. I have no problem with tapping out."

She laughed, "You may surprise yourself, my man. I've observed that guys like to test their tolerance. They are not always smart about it. Sometimes it gets them knocked out! If I advise you 'tap or sleep', believe me, one or the other is going to happen. As I said, I know my stuff."

"Erin, I told the Lord when He suggested this that it would be hard on me, always losing. You're a pro; I know I don't stand much of a chance. I don't want you to let me win; that's dishonest. But I'm not sure how much my damaged ego can take, losing all the time. He told me to tell you my concern, so I am. Am I getting in so far over my head with this that it will destroy me?"

She gathered him in her arms, "*I would never do that to you*. We are not going to compete seriously, love, just work out, scuffle around and play. Tapping out is just a part of the play for us. I'll teach you about what I do, showing you tricks I've learned over the years. Haven't you been curious?"

He nodded.

"You are doing this *for me*. I'll never forget that! I think we're gonna have fun. There's one more thing about this I haven't mentioned yet. You asked me once if wrestling leads to sex. I said no; however, for you and me, it almost certainly *will*. We are husband and wife, so nothing is off limits for us!"

"Well, I might enjoy this after all," he grinned.

"How do you think Mom would respond if I knocked on her door to ask if you could come out to play?" she chuckled.

"Oh, she'd get a laugh out of it, probably tell you yes, you kids go play."

He asked for clarification, "Now, am I your playmate or the toy you will play with?"

"Both!" she giggled.

He protested. "You're gonna cause me to have an identity crisis! Since you were an orphan, I'm not sure if you were ever taught a certain childhood lesson that may directly affect my well-being, as your playmate or your toy. Do you mind if I give you some fatherly advice?"

"Go ahead," she invited expectantly. By this time, she knew him well enough to expect a zinger.

"Okay, it goes like this: if you break your toys and injure your playmates, who's gonna want to play with you?"

She nearly collapsed laughing; if he wasn't holding her, she might have dropped to the floor! For the very first time, she was helpless in his arms, overcome with mirth. Several seconds went by when he wasn't just holding her; he was holding her up.

She eventually recovered, looked at him with adoration, then cracked up again, shaking her head. "I don't believe you!" she finally gasped.

His smile was ear to ear as he held her, watching her laugh.

"Where *were* you all those times I had to throttle back overzealous girls to keep them from injuring my customers? That line would have circumvented so many attitudes that came back at me when I reprimanded them! I could have gotten the point across in such a way that none of them would have been offended. That was simple, brilliant and hilarious!

"My Sweet Talker, *I will do my best* not to injure or break you when I play with you, okay?"

"Thank you! I appreciate that," he said, then kissed her. When he tried to pull back, she hijacked the kiss, spun them around and shoved him down on the bed. He gripped her tightly as he fell, pulling her down on top of him.

She giggled, "What are you doing?"

"Just what you said I would, Genie. Since you are more than I can handle, I'm holding on for dear life!"

"Good call," she chuckled. "Hold on then; I'm gonna see if I can drown you with kisses!"

"Oh, crap!" It was all he got out before he was covered with more affection than a man is prepared to take!

ABOUT THE AUTHOR

Larry Allen Goodyear is a jack of all trades. He has worked in lumber yards, a donut shop, warehouses, driving trucks, cashiering – even participated in laser surgery! A veteran of the U.S. Navy, his most recent occupation is working as a caregiver for the developmentally disabled.

He loves to laugh and get others laughing, saying you can laugh or you can cry, but it's more fun to laugh. Anticipating the sure hope of Heaven, there is no time in his remembrance when Jesus Christ was not his Lord. In childhood he declared he would be a preacher and a scientist! He is neither, but now he is satisfied simply to be faithful.

He now resides in the center of the continental United States in the Ozarks, near his son and grandkids.

www.ingramcontent.com/pod-product-compliance
Lightning Source LLC
Chambersburg PA
CBHW061201170626
46809CB00003B/1199